The Moment Of Intimacy

Collection Of Short Stories

Debajyoti Gupta

ISBN 979-8-89066-934-6

Contents

1

Echoes from the Lake

It was an overcast day. Dev Roy a young boy came to his home town Tripura, after completing his master degree from Assam University, Silchar, the year 2007, the winters of Agartalaare very chilly. Dev took a Master degree in Sociology from Assam University and came to his home town he was planning for doing PhD in Sociology in Assam University after 5 months, when the authority will give him the call to fulfil the required criteria for PhD selection. During his stay in his home town he planned to join a degree college. He was working in Government Degree College in Agartala as a guest Lecturer in Sociology.

When Dev went out of his house in the way to his college, he saw a young girl who was standing near the lake, she was in a sad mood, Dev was standing there and he saw the girl with a red coat, she prepared herself to jump in the lake, as the reason was unknown to Dev, he Shouted, "STAY THERE," and ran toward her and saved her by taking her into his arms, he was carrying a bag, the bag dropped in the ground, the girl picked the bag and gave him. He said, "What happened to you?" She said, "Nothing", but remained silent. At last she said, "Where do you go?" Dev said, "Its college time I have a class now." She said, "Can I come with you." Dev remain silent for a while and said nothing. There after he said, "you may come with me."He went to his college and said the girl to wait, he went to the wash room and washed his face, came out of the wash room and without any hesitation he entered into the class with the girl. The students wished him, GOOD MORNING SIR, Dev also said, "GOOD MORNING LADIES AND GENTELMEN". He asked the girl to sit in a chair which was near the blackboard. All the students were smiling looking at the girl, and some of them are whispering looking at each other.

Dev began his lecture, "Today's Lecture- law of 3 stages defined by August comte, can be said as Theoretical stage, Metaphysical stage and Scientific stage." After a few minutes the girl went out of the room without saying anything to Dev, she also left her coat in the class. When she went out Dev was looking outside through the window to find the girl. Where is she going? Dev said to his students, "You all just care on with the question I am giving you now. Please write the questions, *Emergence of Sociology in the west or write about the protestant ethics and the spirit of capitalism? Write the answers I am coming right now."*

Dev went outside the building, and was looking for that girl to return her coat. A female worker of the college came towards him and said, "Sir, any problem," her name was Anne. Dev said, "I was just looking for a girl, did you saw her". Anne said, "No, I came just now, I did not saw anybody." Dev said, "Ok, you may go."

By the time the students were making noise in the class room. They all were busy with useless talks between themselves, just frolicking and making noise. At that moment the vice principal Miss Roy entered the class room. She said loudly, "WHAT THE NOISE HERE? Where is Dev?" One of the girls wears a smile and said, "A girl came with him, I think she is now waiting outside and he might have followed her."

Miss Roy was surprised; she was silent for a while and said, "Did he give you any work." The girl said, "Yes, two questions." Miss Roy said, "Then why you all shouting so much do your work." All the students became quite and they became engaged in their works.

Miss Roy came out of the class and was searching for Dev in the college campus, but he was not found. At last Miss Roy call himin his cell phone Dev received the call, "Hello", Miss Roy said, " Hello Dev, Where are you?", Dev said, "I am near the lake, will you please look after my class this time, I will come next day." Saying this Dev rejected the call. Miss Roy was surprised; she was thinking his health is not good so he went away.

Basically, Dev is a good teacher, but, little bit boring, however looks good and this attracts other towards him. He went back to his house as his parents were waiting for him, His asked him, "how was your class this today? He replied, "Fine", his mother said, "A letter came today I think it came from one of your hostel friends."

Dev opened the envelop and saw it was the letter from his friend named Birancy Hazarika his room wall mate in the hostel. There is no word as room wall mate there is room mate but in Assam University hostels there are single and double rooms so students staying in single rooms they used to say the person staying next to them as wall mates.

Dear Dev,

Hope you are fine. Today I am writing you this letter to tell you I am

studying in Calcutta University. I took the same subject as my subject

was Education. I know that you are going to do PhD in sociology

after few months, you keep in touch with me good bye.

Your friend
Birancy (Bishu)

Reading this letter Dev went back to his hostel, where he was for 2 years. Birancy was his wall mate, Dev used to stay in a single room; he was only busy in himself. He calls Birancy as Bishu which is very funny.

Dev when he could manage time he talks with his friends in the hostel on phone, namely panna, pronoy kamie, gaurav, Amar, Krishna kant, Ravi, Ranjan, Pallab, jasim whom he miss always.

It was night, 9 o clocks, by the time it became foggy all around. Even the sights of the near distance show hazy. Everywhere it was full of Mist. He had his dinner and was sitting near the window and was thinking about the girl, whose face is still haunting him. At that moment he got a phone call from the Vice principal Miss Roy, Dev received the call. "Hello". Miss Roy said, "Dev good evening, how you are, I thought you are not keeping well." Dev said, "No madam, I am alright." Miss Roy said, "No, Dev I felt you are sick anyhow, for that you left the class, but, who was that girl with you." Dev said, "Who said you about it." Miss Roy said, "The students were telling me." Dev simply said, "I just meet her near the lake." Miss Roy said, "ok, I see, I just call you tomorrow you have a class at 11:30." Dev said, "Ok, Madam I will come on time.

Net morning, Dev took his breakfast and went to the college. He entered the staff room; there he saw some of his colleagues were looking at him and giggling. Dev took his seat opened the book and was reading. It was fixed 11 am for his lecture. He went to the class delivered his lecture, and went outside the college building and was sitting near the play ground. One of his colleagues came towards him and sat silently besides him, her name was Shelly. She was a teacher of English literature. She asked Dev, "How are you"? Dev replied in a slow voice, "fine." She further asked, "I hope the class is over." Dev said," Yes, and you?" She said. "Yes, So when you are leaving to pursue your PhD program." Dev said, "When I will receive a call from the university for PhD selection exams, may be after 5 months or might be early."Shelly said, "I think you will leave your job." Dev said, "yeah, of course, it's just a per time job, feeling bored at home and it's just means to pass time simply, nothing more." Shelly said, "I am getting married after 3 months, you are invited." Dev said, "Yeah off course." Shelly said, "You know it is our love marriage." Dev said, "That's great." Shelly said. "Love at first side." Dev said. "For that it's called crushes happens ones in a life time." Shelly said, "All you said right, do you have any crush" Dev said. "No never. I just write stories about it, so sometimes like that." Shelly said, "I know I read some of your stories which you had published I nicely read it, but, I found something about that you had visited a temple in Tripura on Kharchi festival can you please tell something about it."Dev said, "last year between July to August I visited the festival, this festival is worshipped of the dynasty diety of people living in Tripura, involves 14 Gods. The word Kharchi is derived from the word khar or khathar which means Sin or chi actual meaning is clearing, as you can say cleaning sin of the people or the kingdom. Kharchi puja is performed after 15 days of Ama Pechi." Shelly said.

"What is Ama Pechi?" Dev said, "According to the legends of Tripura Ama Pechi means Menstruation of the mother goddess or mother earth. Among the local people of Tripura there lies a belief that the Menstruation period is to be regarded as unholy so the soil is not been digged in that time, so no type of activities are to be performed in that period by any women who is passing through menstruation. So the kharchi puja is performed to wash up the sin which is to be caused by the menstruation. This is why it is performed for seven consecutive days at Chadhaa Devata temple. People from tribal to non tribal gather in that festival and offer fruits, goats, bullocks, sweets etc as Prasadh, a large fair is also organized in that occasion. People seek for their welfare as well as the welfare of the society and the state in general, and the festival gets over."

Shelly said, "Very interesting, I think I will visit this festival next year. Dev I heard the king who used to sacrificed innocent boys in the temple do you know the name."

Dev said, "yes, his name was King Govindo Mynikya,ok, let me leave it is nearly 12: 30, good bye." Shelly said, "Good bye Dev."

Dev was on way to home, at that time a girl came towards him. Dev was surprised to look at the girl it was the girl whom he met near the lake. Dev said, "Hey, what are you doing here, where you went yesterday, I took you in classroom and you suddenly disappeared, you know I was waiting for you, looking your way. What's your name?" She was smiling and said, "My name is Adriana. Yesterday you saw me I was there by the lake side waiting for nothing, but, you thought I was going to jump and kill myself. But it was not so, by the way I liked you coming towards me and holding my hands, I saw in you a very true person" Dev said, "What do you mean?" Adriana said, "Nothing. Extraordinary, I can feel your pulse well, my house is near your house if you like you may visit my house, I stay with my aunt."

Dev said, "then where is your home, tell me exact location". Adriana said, "I stay with my aunt." Dev said, "Ok, good bye, I am late for my home." Adriana said, "Can you take me to your college tomorrow? I wish a further visit there once again." Dev said, "Why?" Adriana said, "No, just for no reason "Dev said "ok, I have your coat left with me, tomorrow I will give you if you want." Adriana said, "all right, that means we will meet tomorrow." Dev said, "I hope so."

Dev went back to home. His mother said, "A letter came from the University, I think from one of your friends." His father asked, "Why you are so late?" Dev said, "I was just busy taking classes."His father said. "I see."

He took the letter in his hand and begins to read it; the letter was from one of his friends from the hostel Prakash Dubey.

Dear Dev da,

Hope you are fine. We all are missing you very much. Pronoy, Kamai, Amar, Ranjan, Saurav both of them and Deepak were asking about you. When we were in the hostel you used to visit our room each and every one of ours and gossip with us. Actually our discussion the same what teens used to discuss about girls who lookspretty and adult movies. Sometimes we know that you feel bored but you want to join us. Tinkal was telling about you, he forgot some of his boxing punches which you used to teach him but one thing we all remember your simple punch has created a great impact in our mind. Suraj Mauriga was also talking about you to gaurav, ravi, and others they all miss you very much. You remember he used to keep bamboo sticks or shoes in front of your door steps when you were not there, he really miss you. Mohit, Abilek, Bhaskar, was talking about you if you come here again we all will be happy. When we all go to the ground to play cricket we all miss your batting performance I, kamai, Suresh and Pranay was talking about you how much runs you used to score, we still find your absence in our play ground, because you are better than us, what you used to say "THE BEST IN THE WORLD," for that reason every one used to call you Jessie Ryder. Panna Sanjeeb, Sikander, Pronoy and Kamie were talking about you what all fun we all used to have. Do you remember your best friend David; he is now a teacher in a school. We all are here for one month in this hostel, after that we all are leaving, hope you will come here for PhD but we all will be not here, we all have a leave unfortunately.

Today, Mukunda Hasarika told me and Paul thakuria that when he was moving through your room he thought you are in the room, he knocked the door, but it was someone else. We still feel your absence in our hostel, our cook Subash Sharma, remash, Nakul and rejesh has left the hostel they also told me about you. We all miss you. Hope we meet you again in life.

Yours Friend
Prakash Dubey

After reading the letter he went back to his University where he was for 2 years. Actually he was not present in the University, Department or in the Hostel but his presence is felt, when someone leaves a place it doesn't means he left the place for ever, we left behind the marks of us. He may not be present in the hostel but his marks are present, the marks can be found only by going in that place again. He was absorbed in thought and the night passed.

Next morning he got ready for class. He saw Adriana to come forward and approached him and said, "Wow, you do not forget to bring my coat. May I accompany you up to college?" Dev said, "ok, but not in class room."Adriana said, "You go to your class I will be in the campus waiting for you." Dev said, "Ok, you may come." Dev said, "Adriana you stay with whom in this place." Adriana said, "I stay with my aunt, she is a doctor, now she is in her clinic she had retired 5 years before, she will come at 5pm." Dev said, "Fine, Dev went to the college with Adriana all the students were waiting for him, Dev entered the college building. The Vice Principal saw Dev, with the girl, she said, "Oh, you came Please go and take the class the students are waiting for you," but Miss Roy did not said anything about Adriana After 1 hour he came out of his class room. Adriana was waiting outside for him. Dev came outside of the college building and he saw Adriana was sitting in the college park; he wet towards her and said, "So you saw everything or something is left behind." Adriana said, "Yes, I saw" Dev said, "So, let's leave now." Adriana was sitting in the branch for 1 hour waiting for him, but Dev did not know that. On the way to home Adriana asked him, "Dev have you any girlfriend."Dev was surprised. He said,

"Why?"Adriana said, "no, just for no reason", Dev said, no, I do not have any girlfriend and I am not interested for so."Adriana said, "But, I read some of your stories about love." Dev said, "Who gave you my book, you do not live here." Adriana said," no, my aunt is a very big fan of yours, she reads your stories, she also knows yours parents very well." Dev said, "So what is her name?" Adriana said, "Dr. Ranjana Dey, you please meet her today she will be very happy to see you, please." Dev said, "No, today I cannot meet her I will have to go to home." Adriana said, "Please,you stay at least for 5 minutes she will be very happy to see you." Dev said, "Let's see". Dev entered to the house of Adriana's aunt, Dr Ranjana opened the door and saw Dev she was very happy to see him. She began talking with Dev. Dr Ranjana said, "Adriana why do not you prepare coffee for him." Adriana said, "Yeah off course." Adriana went to the kitchen to prepare coffee for Dev.

Miss Ranjana said, "Dev you know I leave alone in this house. After few days she will also leave, really I feel very happy when she comes here." Dev said, "You did not marry." Dr Ranjana smiled and said, "No dear. I did not find any one to choose." Dev said, "Similarly I think not to get married, because

I could not find any girl whom I deserve and such match will not be found anywhere." Dr Ranjana said, "No, God has made some one for each and every one, I did not find anyone that's my misfortune but, I know you will get someone matching your choice." Dev said, "How, it is possible I do not understand." Dr Ranjana said, "Remember my words. When you will meet that girl she will inspires you to fall in love, until your every sense is touched by her, you inhale her, you taste her, you can see your unborn children in her eyes and at last your heart has found a home to live, your life begins with her and without her it surely ends."

Adriana came with the coffee. Dev said. "Ok, let's see". It's time for Dev to go home. Adriana came towards the door steps with Dev and said. "Bye, good night."

Dev went home and thinking about Dr Ranjana what she said to him. Her words inspired him very much.

He was sitting near the window side of the balcony of his door and was thinking about his university which he left;sometimes ago-*it was a foggy morning in January, the morning which took away the atmospheric beauty in its arms. I was standing near the hostel where the building light made me look at my reflection instead of theMerchandise. Itwas annoying to stand in my own way particularly since the whole thing was like an allegory of the way I usually stood by me and I was about to make my way inside through the shadowy funnels of my hands, when behind my reflection it reminded me of the threatening storm shadow that changed the world the figure of my lecturer, who used to teach me in the college De Fillip Sam, nobody liked him to do the class but I liked it, may be because he was a true person who used to tell me never to give up and others used to hate him because he tells useless words about sexuality. This strange man was a man of his words, he was my teacher but seems to me as a stranger but better than my school teachers, those who used to keep me in the beneath, used to have idiotic ideologies about life, but some of them were perfect.*

Next morning a letter came to his house from one of his friends from hostel. Dev received the letter from the letter box and opened it and it was the letter from his friend Kamie, he started reading the letter.

Dear Dev

Hey Dev da, hope you are fine, very long time to see you. It hadbeen early evening, through the open balcony door a light warmwind brought the sounds and smells of a dying summer day, and ifthis soft wave of brightness could have been enjoyed in freedomand oblivion, it could have been a moment of happiness. If only asharp, ruthless wind had whipped the rain against the Window pane,I remember you were there hope so, but not, I love someone when I

was young I am studying law which deals with rules, the girl whomI loved she did not understood about love, true love, not about sexfor a while, we all miss you very much, we all played footballtournament there I missed you very much, I felt your absence in ourplayground, I will send you the pictures of our tournament in youremail. You remember Nancy our friend she is not well now a days. It has been heard that she is pregnant, she was having an affair and now it happened, love is what we know as it is, hope we meet again, good bye.

Yours friend

Kamie

Next morning Dev went to college and, when he finished his lecture he was on his way to home. At that moment he meets Adriana. She said, "It drizzles" and brought an umbrella, She said, "come I will reach you to your house." Dev said." please do not worry, I can manage it well." Suddenly the wind blew away the umbrella from Adriana's hand and it was raining very heavily. Adriana said." Dev it is winter, you may fall sick, please come to my house, please, please I say PLEASE, when the rain ceases you leave." Dev had no other choose but to listen to Adriana. He went to her house. Dev said, "Where is your aunt." Adriana said, "She is engaged in some meeting and before leaving she told me she will come late."Dev said, "Well", Adriana was drenched in the rain, and Dev eyes were looking at her head to toe, she was looking very beautiful. Dev could re collect what was said to him by Dr Ranjana. At that moment Dev did not restrained himself and came close to Adriana. Adriana smiled and said, "Do you want coffee?" Dev said, "No, I want to say you something Adriana which I feel now it's all from the core of my heart". Adriana said, "Say it freely."

Dev said, "Adriana you know, in our younger life we search for someone, someone who can complete us, we choose partners change partners. We dance in every bit of drum and hope something cheering;

some perfect is waiting for us. I know it's a very hard moment, I know at some point both of us will come out of this moment, but if I do not ask you to be mine, I will regret it for the rest of my life, because you are only perfect for me. It is for the first time I say it to a girl like you. Believe me Adriana; I am saying to a girl for the first and for the last time, I love you, you complete me."After that tears rolling from her eyes, she came toward him and hugs him kissed him in his lips. Adriana said. "I love you too, from the day I saw you."

Adriana took him to the room and closed the door. He undressed her it was the first time he saw someone completely a naked beauty after watching all those porn movies. He sucked her boobs, kissed her navel, they both were kissing each other using their tongue for stimulation, he cannot control his hard erection. Adriana said, "Please stop I am going through my periods now." Dev do not know what is periods but his friend used to discuss about the periods in girls in the hostel, he also remember in his class one of his friend named Nazima told him that she was not feeling well now a days than Dev asked her what has happened to you she replied she was passing through periods. After a moment his figures touched in her vagina he can feel the blood spot now he came to know what periods is, but, he moved his figure gently on that area." Adriana said, "Dev fuck me harder much harder till I reach the climax." Dev said, "It's coming, my cum can I cum over your body." Adriana said, "No, just inside me." Dev said, "I am not using any protection." Adriana said, "No need I want to feel you from inside just do it." Dev ejaculated inside her after that she said, "Its great, thanks Dev I enjoyed a lot, with great orgasm I love you Dev." Dev said, "I love you too."Next morning he went to Adriana's home. Dev knocked the door, Dr Ranjana opened the door. She said, "Aunty Can I meet Adriana." Dr Ranjana said, "Last night she went, I asked her why are you leaving so early it was midnight, she did not told me anything she just gave me a letter to hand over you."

Dev simply went out of the house, he was very sad; he opened the letter of Adriana and begins reading it:

Dear Dev,

I am leaving forever, and, I want to say you good bye, but can't say, do not have the habit to say so. I know what happened last night, I cannot explain, but it was not that, it was belongings of each other. This temptation was not only for a while but for me it is forever. I pray to God you always be happy. Hope to meet you again during the span of life, if not, there will be someone else very beautiful who will give you love and support you life, but if we meet again, it willbe in a different place and in different time, as different individuals, but, I will always love you.

Yours
Adriana

Tears rolled down silently from Dev's eyes. He went back to home and his parents said, "Your call letter for PhD exams came very early, you will have to leave next month." Dev said, "Yes, I will." His mother said, "but you will miss your all friends."

Dev said, "No, I will get them for one and half months in the hostel." His mother said, "Ok, that's good." His father said, "go and take some rest I think you are tired." Dev said, "I just want to go out for some time." His father said, "Where?" Dev said, "In the lake side." His mother said, "Ok, do not be late." Dev said, "I will not be late."

Dev went to the lake side and was looking at the lake water; the lake was surrounded by mist where the echoes were coming from the lake. It's all about Adriana, after few minutes it began to look hazy and Dev thought he will not find out a way out so suddenly and easily.

2

One Evening

It was an evening 3 friends were sitting in their room in the hostel and were talking with each other. The year 2012, Silchar in Assam University. Debarun was little bit separate from them, he remain busy in his works including studies, next day Debarun had to change his room and to go to a single room. It was dazzling and a rainy night. It was the month of October and after 20 days the students will leave the hostel for their Durja puja festival vacation. All the students were in the hostel and the warder went out to his friend's house to take alcohol. Debarun was new to the hostel and was saying to Paul, Debarun said, "Paul you have a cream." Paul said, "No." Samuel said, "I have a gel cream." Debarun said, "What is that gel cream?" Paul smiled, Samuel said, "I used it for masturbating when I watch porn." Debarun said, "You will never change." Paul was laughing and said. "Season changes but he will never change." Debarun said, "I do not have any cream tomorrow is a holiday I think on Monday I have to go to the Silchar town." Samuel said. "If you visit to the Silchar town please visit the dirty area of 14 number." Debarun said. "What is that?" Paul was smiling. Samuel said, "Paul did you have your laptop with internet connection." Paul said, "I have my laptop what you want to see." Samuel said, "Nothing I just want to download porn." Paul said, "day after day you are becoming very wicked." Samuel said. "Please give me your laptop for a while please." Paul gave his laptop to him. Samuel said, "Paul how is you crush Nafiza." Debarun said, "Who is Nafiza?". Samuel said, "Actually Nafisa is a girl from Paul law department they both read in the same class, Samuel likes her but she has a boyfriend Raj actually when Paul looks at her he becomes horny and directly go to the bathroom for shaking, *ha ha ha ha.*" Paul said, "Samual you bitch stop making fun of me." Samuel said, "You only told me that last week and you said Nafisa with her boyfriend Raj went to the toilet and shaked his penis for masterbation."Debarun said, " You all are very nasty,ok, let me go to sleep, I am very tired today, good night." Paul said, good night."

Next morning Debarun woke up in the morning and was standing near the balcony and watching the morning view. Dilip and Aziz came to him and were saying him that they are going to play cricket now. Mohit said. "Debarun da we are going to play cricket now you please come. Debarun said, "I am coming." Aziz said. "Wait we all will go together please wait for us." Debarun said. "Come." Aziz said. "Please wait of sometime let us talk for a while look Basu also came." Debarun said. "Basu you will not play today." Basu said, "I will." Debarun said, "So let's go to the field." Basu said, "After some time I just had my breakfast."Aziz said, "I told Debarun he also had his breakfast just now, let's have a talk." Debarun said. "Ok." Aziz said, "Debarun you ever saw porn." Dilip and Basu were laughing. Debarun said, "What non sense you are sayingto me for that you told me to stay here." Dilip said, "no no Debarun da, just having fun you know I never watch this things how you feel jumping on one another sucking and fucking the anal putting the dick in the mouth so disgusting and erasing the juice." Basu said, "Dilip how do you know so much." Dilip said, "I read it in the books." Suran shouted from the back. Suran said, "Ooii Dilip sala beti chud you are a real ass hole shut up you all are trying to spoil Debarun da, Basu da and Aziz da also doing the same thing." Aziz said, "No I was just taking a class of Debarun." Debarun said, "I am not interested in all your non sense."

Suren said, "Debarun da you know this Dilip used to download all this porn videos from our department he is so nasty, do not make fun of Debarun da you have no idea what he did to Kuldeep and if you do not believe asked Kuldeep he stay next to your room. "Dilip said, "You shut up Suran, Debarun da I watch I like to watch I say you to watch what this non sense Suran is saying." Debarun said, "oak I am leaving I am going to the field." Basu said, "Wait I am coming."Debarun went to the field.

Next morning Debarun woke up early and went to Silchar town. It took 1 hour to go to Silchar from his University. He went to Silchar in his auntie's house, and had the lunch his aunty told him to stay for the night with her in the house and the next morning he can leave to go to the University, but he said he will go to the University by tonight as possible. Debarun went to the market and brought certain things what he wanted to buy some medicines espically his hypertension medicines which he started to take before 1 year. At that moment a sudden wind was blowing and it began to rain.

It was a heavy shower. He was in a cafe sitting and drinking a cup of coffee, no one was there he was thinking when the rain will stop and he can go to the

University. At that moment his aunty rang him in his mobile told him to come in her house his uncle was waiting for him. But Debarun said he will come after the rain stops.

Debarun saw a girl in the coffee shop she was sitting just opposite to him. The girl said, "Can you please give me your pen for a while." Debarun gave her the pen, the girl wrote something on a piece of paper in Bengali and gave him the pen back. The girl said, "What is your name." Debarun said. "My name is Debarun and yours." The girl said, "My name is Elie." Debarun said, "What do you do?" Elie said, "I am a student I study in a college you do not think at this moment we were sharing the same flame."Debarun said, "I do not think so." Elie said, "May be an intimate way." Debarun said, "I do no think so what intimate is there can you say." Elie said, "no, I think when you gave me your pen my hand touched you and yours mine." Debarun said, "You study in which college." Elie said, "Women College." Debarun said, "Which year." Elie said, "2nd year."Debarun said, "okk, I see." Elie said, "What you do?" Debarun said, "I am a PhD scholar in the University." Elie said, "You donot think at this moment we are sharing the same flame." Debarun said, "What are you saying I cannot understand." Elie said, "An intimate way." Debarun said, "No, not intimate it was the candle burning in front of us on the table." Elie said, "No, I think when you gave me the pen. my hand touched yours and mine yours that way." Debarun said, "You study in college you said." Elie said, "I lied I do not study in college." Debarun said, "What you do?" Elie said, "I am a call girl and have my own website." Debarun said, "Why you said me wrong things." Elie said, "Just to know you better." Both of them were discussing in the coffee house. Elie said, "You believe in soul mate, finding some on the better half." Debarun said, "I cannot accept this type of questions from you." Elie said, "We are human beings and have emotions and limits." Debarun said, "I know". Elie said, "It is better to fuck someone, a stranger you did not know him and you hardly see his face." Debarun said, "Being a call girl you understand many things, but I am not interested to fuck you." Elie said, "Yes, I know but sometimes we get cheated from guys whom we know and want to spend the rest of our life with him, so it is better to make love with them whom we did not know, Now a day's time has changed we see little girl giving a blowjob and fucking her uncle she is much more exited to taste the cum of a older man than her same age boyfriend, everyone wants a experienced sex partner."Debarun said, "You can make many good stories." Elie siad, "there are many stories, have you visited the 14 number area of Silchar." Debarun said, "please stop your nonsence." Elie said, "Why so angry, actually I am saying because you know this is a area of prostitutes and near there the area a story was there a girl use to walk at night to find clients, she was very attactive and she used to have sex like you young people and if any one doesnot satisfied her she used to cut their penis and fry it in her kitten and eat that, but one day one police officer killed her or she was going to kill a innocent boythat boy was unable to satisfied her."Debarun said, "Ok I am leaving its time for me." Eile said, "Nice meeting you mark my words, I also have to leave to meet my client."Debarun went out of the coffee shop to his aunty s house. His aunty name was Radha, she were waiting for him. Radha said, "Come for your dinner, I and your uncle were waiting for you, Debarun said, "I was in the coffee shop it was raining for a long time." Radha said, "I know finish your lunch and go to sleep, tomorrow your uncle will drop you to the university."Debarun went to sleep and woke up the next morning and went to his University to his hostel.

Debarun brought his new laptop and everyone in the hostel came to see his laptop. Debarun knows a very little the use of it. He calls his friend Krishna to help him out. He used to stay in his opposite room. One day Krishna was not there in his room, so he calls Pranoy one of his best friend he was junior to him but Pronoy see him as his elder brother and respects him but sometimes makes fun with him. Pranoy came to his room and said, "Debarun da I came from my house Tinsukia a district in Assam today I heard that you brought a new laptop, I told you will need a laptop." Debarun said, "I know you please help me I don't have an email ID please make it for me." Pronoy said, "oak, no problem do not worry after that you create a face book account now a day's everything is www.facebook.com." Debarun said, "Means you see your face in a book." Pronoy said, "You don't understand anything." Debarun said, "Make my email Id I need it argent."After few minutes Pronoy said, "See your email ID it has been created.   debarunsen1234@gmail.com."Debarun said, "Thank you very much." Pronoy said, "What thank you,you brought a laptop do something with it what is that bore." Debarun said, "What bore?" Pronoy said. "Listen I am opening a website, look." Debarun said, "What" Pronoy said, "Goggle chat." Debarun said, "Means I will talk with goggle." Pronoy said, "You are totally bullshit, look at this website." Debarun said. "What website?" Pronoy said, "www.naughtyamerica.com." Debarun said. "What is this?" Pronoy said, "Wait it is opening." The webpage got open and Debarun said, "CLOSE ITT, nonsense, stupid." Pronoy said, "Clam down silent nothing wrong." Debarun said, "you get up I understood everything you stupid boy." Pronoy said, "Oak I am leaving if you have any problem you call me." Debarun said, "no need to call you I understood everything bye."Pronoy was smiling and went out of his room shooting and laughing.

From that day he always remains busy in the computer for some or the other work. He just looks at the laptop and read the daily news all over India as well as his place Tripura. He found that in a big house of Silchar a old lady was killed but it was still a mystery even now, some of the people says that the murderer was not yet been found, Silchar is a place where murder take place in a very peaceful way and none of the criminals are caught. One night it was nearly 12 am Debarun was busy in his laptop searching the goggle. A message came to him with a sound *pipppppp* he was surprised what was that? He then opened the massage and a girl wants to chat with him, he immediately rejected the call but again the sound was made. He thought let him look into the matter. He opened the chat box and saw a very beautiful girl in front of him the girl cannot see him but he can see the girl. The girl asked him, "How are you?" He said, "Who are you?" The girl said, "I am your friend." Debarun said, "But I do not know you." The girl said, "My name is Natasha." Debarun said, "So." Natasha smiled and said, "What is your name?" Debarun said, "My name is Debarun." Natasha said, "very nice name where from you Debarun." Debarun said, "I am from Silchar." Natasha said, "Where is Silchar?" Debarun said, "It is in India." Natasha said, "it is nice meeting you Debarun." Debarun said, "Where are you from?" Natasha said, "I am fromMoscow in Russia." Debarun said. "You are an Indian." Natasha said, "My father was an Indian but my mother was Russian my father used to work here as a bank manger so I am living here and studying here in Moscow University." Debarun said. "What subject?" Natasha said, "Economics."Debarun said, "It's good." All day and night he chats with Natasha; it seems that she was a part of his life. Every time when he opens the laptop he waits for Natasha when she will be online. He was in a great joy it seems that he had fallen in love with her.

In the department Debarun said to one of his friends, "Oii, Rupali you did your masters in geography." Rupali said, "no my Bachelor degree honours was in Geography and masters in Sociology, but,from Sociology why are you asking me about Geography." Debarun said, "No, I just want to know that what the climate is in Russia." Rupali said, "You want to go to Russia." Debarun said, "No, I am just asking "Rupali said, "may be cold." Debarun said, "you do not know actually what the climate is." Rupali said. "Just like that." Debarun said, "I do not know how you passed your Bachelors."One night Debarun was talking with Natasha in the webcam. Natasha said, "Oak. Debarun can I see your face for a while." Debarun said, "Oak but how." Natasha said, "When I give you a call you just accept." Debarun said, "But in front of you I am a very ordinary man." Natasha said, "may be but I respect you just click accept." Natasha gave a call and when he was going to accept the call he can hear the screaming of Natasha she was shouting with a man in front of the web cam and calling for help. Debarun was watching this in his laptop. Suddenly the man took out a knife from his jacket and killed Natasha. He was shocked my watching this he also saw the man face, the night was passed he did not slept he was sitting near his laptop with a shocking face.

The next morning his mobile was ringing it was the call from his home but he did not picked it up. After a while his parents gave a call to his friend Utpal whose room was next to him. Utpal said, "Uncle he is in the hostel in his room you please hold on let me check it out." Utpal went to his room the room was locked from inside, Utpal thought he was sleeping. Utpal said, "Uncle I think he is sleeping he will call you when he will woke up do not worry I will tell him."

For 2 hours, the door remained locked. Debarun did not open the door Utpal came toward the door and knocked but no response from him then all the boys came and pushed the door the door got open. They saw Debarun head was lying in the table in front of his laptop."All the hosteller took him to the health centre the doctor said he is alright something shocking happened to him. His parents called him in Utpal's mobile but he did not say anything he remained silent. After that he always remains silent in the hostel does not talk to anyone which he used to do, he was a funny guy sometimes remain serious and funny. He remains in his room in silent never touch his laptop, even he do not go to attain his PhD classes in his department. His teachers were also asking for him, his friends call him but he never attain their call. In his department his professor told to Utpal to call Debanun to attain the Seminar which was going too held the next day and after 7 days the University will be closed for Durga puja and it will be opened after the Diwali.

Utpal and Pronoy went to his hostel and knocked in Debarun's room. Debarun opened the door, Utpal said, and "how are you now?" Debarun didn't have any reply. Utpal said, "What happened to you are you sick you tell me anything wrong with you." Debarun said, "I do not want to stay here anymore Utpal I just want to leave my research works and go back to my house." Utpal said, "Why anyone said you anything you tell me." Debarun said, "no one said me nothing. I do not want to stay here, nightmares would chase me in my sleep, and I am feeling in my own eyes right now, my heart is pounding, my legs are trembling, and confusion is erupting in my stomach." Pronoy said, "legs are trembling, heart is pounding and stomach problems; in this age, I think you should avoid eating fast foods, is very bad for health. Debarun said, "Shut up Pronoy I am not joking." "Utpal said, "Oak, Pronoy keep quiet, Debarun listen tothe music in your laptop you will feel better." Debarun shouted and said, "Do not switch on the laptop it's a killer." Utpal was shocked he said what happened. Debarun said. "You please leave me along." Utpal said. "OK, I am leaving I just came here to tell you Professor Behara told me to inform you tomorrow there will be a seminar in the department a guest will come from abroad you please come on time."

Next morning Debarun went to his department to attain the seminar. The seminar was started all the guest had arrived to the department hall. A announcement was made by Professor Behera, he said, "here comes our special guest from Russia my friend Professor Raj Sen. form Moscow university and he is going to join our Department as a new Professor." When professor Raj entered the room every on stood up Debarun saw professor Raj and was shockingly afraid and shouted and said, "HE IS A KILLER" Everyone surprised to hear that and also professor Behera, Professor Raj was standing in front of the table and was normal. Professor Behera said, "Debarun what nonsense you are talking about shut up." Debarun said, "sir, I saw him killed a girl." Professor Behera said, "You are suspended and do not show your face again, Utpal take him away from here or I will rusticate him." Debarun said, "No I am saying the truth" Utpal said, "Debarun come I will listen to you." Utpal brought out him from the room. Professor Behere said, "Professor Raj I am sorry for that I do not know what he is saying he is sick for few days." Professor Raj said, "No it's oak, let's start our discussion."

Utpal brought him out of the department and took him to the canteen. Utpal said, "What wrong is with you Debarun, I know you are sick for few days but you are taking a mental stress." Debarun said, "I am saying the truth I saw this man killing a girl in my laptop in front of me." Utpal said, "Again you started." Debarun said, "You do not believe me come to the hostel." Both of them went to their hostel, Debarun opened his laptop and shown him the girl and told him that she was murdered by that man Professor Raj. Utpal said, "You have any evidence that hekilled her ". Debarun said. "No I had seen him killing her with a knif, he tried to rape her and while she was trying to escape he killed her Utpal said, "I believe you but we need proof without that everything is impossible." Debarun said, "So what can I do now." Utpal said, "I will tell you what to do, tomorrow we will go to meet professor Raj in the guest house of our University and you will tell him sorry." Debarun said, "No I cannot do that." Utpal said, "You have to or you cannot proof that you are innocent. "Debarun said, "all right I will do it."

On the other side Professor Raj in the university guest house was thinking how this boy saw him killing Natasha, he was thinking to kill Debarun but he cannot do so because he is in another country and if he kills him then everyone will come to know that Debarun was right.

Next morning Debarun went up early, it took a little bit of time for him to wake up, not because he was sleepy but his mind was elsewhere. He mind was struck on Professor Raj why he killed Natasha. Utpal came to his room and said. "Oak are you ready, let's go." Debarun said, "oak let's go." Uptal and Debarun went to the university guest house. At that moment they meet with Professor Behera he said, "oak, what are you both doing here?" Utpal said, "Actually sir, Debarun realised his fault he came here to say sorry to Professor Raj" Professor Behera said, "He should say that a very bad behavoir he did that day for the first time it happened in the University a guest have been insulted badly." Debarun did not say anything but he was trying to say but Utpal stopped him. Professor Behera said, "Oak next Monday your puja vacation starts, meet you all after the vacation." Saying these things he went from that place. Both of them knocked in the room of Professor Raj, he opened the room and said, "Both of you here." Utpal said, "Sir, my friend came here to say you sorry." Professor Raj said, "Come inside." Debarun told sorry to him and said, "Sir Can I use your toilet." Professor Raj said. "Yes that's the way." Debarun went to the toilet and was thinking whether he is wrong has he saw something wrong at that moment he saw ajacket when Nathasha was killed the killer wore that jacket, and also he got a dairy he opened the diary and had a look he heard that Professor Raj was calling him, he took the dairy inside his shirt and came from there and said, "Sir, it was nice meeting you we have to leave now." Professor Raj said, "Oak bye." They both came out of the house and Debarun said, "I got a diary Utpal." Utpal said, "Whose diary." Debarun said. "Professor Raj. "They both went to the hostel and opened the diary to read, it was written there:

DIARY 1

June 1, 2009

I was a professor in the University of Moscow, came new to this city and fallen in love with a girl in the class named Natasha and every one used to call her Nikka. I do not know how it happened but it happened. I had a habit in the night may be of chatting in the night time with the girls who wears a panty or a underwear and I cover my face with a mask and starts chatting in front of the webcam. I like to do this; this gives me a great pleasure. But, one day everything was changed, when the day ended when I saw Natasha entering my classroom. As if I can feel the presence of Susan, the girl whom I used to love in the school. I am a guy whose age is 55 at present. But I feel my pulses to 20- 25 age boy. I know Natasha was 22 years old. So what I wanted to fuck a girl younger than me. So I helped her in her studies, I knew she need my help even though I used to help her.

May 2, 2010

One day I proposed her, but she did not accepted and she said she respects me as her teacher, nothing else more than that, I do not liked that never. Many girls who were my students I fucked them but she was special to me. So when I see her my dick bulge up.

DIARY 2

July 10, 2011

I remember Susan in the school bus I came towards her and took my sit in front of her. I cannot say what brings me closer to her was it the sweet smell of the perfume which comes out of her dress or her brown knees. I think the fragmented of soap force me to go in front of her.

October 5, 2012

The same thing I found in Natasha. One night I saw her chatting in the webcam 1 do not know with whom I came from the back and said her to marry me. She was shocked to see me she said "NO" and was shooting, screaming. I forced her to make love with me, but she was trying to escape I brought a knife in my jacket and killed her, is that what she deserve and took the body and thrown it in the river Volga. No one can find the evidence. So I came from Russia to India to escape if there are no clues found. I like what 1 want to do and if not then there are severe consequences what is paid by this foolish girl Natasha everything was alright but Debarun a boy from India saw that I came to know it now, he saw me I killed her that time Natasha was chatting with Debarun but I did not knew that if necessary he has to pay the same price.

Utpal said, "See you are right he killed her and now you are his target I have to inform this matter to the local police of Dargakuna " Debarun said, "Do not go now because it is too late now it is 8 pm." Utpal said, "So what it is the matter of your life I have to inform the police." Debarun said, "Oak I will go with you." Utpal said, "No, I will go alone if you go he can attack you, you please stay here I will come back after 1 hour you keep the diary with you." Saying these things Utpal went to the Police station, 2 hours had passed but he did not return, Debarun was worried for him, he called in his mobile but it was switch off. After few

minutes a call came to his mobile Debarun received call the call was made from his friend Utpal mobile, Debarun said, "Utpal you came where are you" From

Utpal mobile a sound came, "1 am professor Raj your friend Utpal is with me bring my dairy or I will kill him bring it now." Debarun was shocked and said, "I am bringing do not do anything to him."Professor Raj said, "Oak." Debarun went to Professor Raj with the diary and gave him the diary, Professor Raj said. "your friend Utpal before going to the police station I caught him and took him in my gun point but now I have to kill you both with my gun because both of you know my secret." When Professor Raj was going to shot them.Suddenly the police came and shoot in his hand and the revolver fall down, the Debarun's hostel warden and some of his friends Aaziz, Dilip and Pronoy were with him. Professor Raj was arrested with all the evidence and he was send to Russia. Debarun said to his warden, "Sir you called the police." His name was Professor Deepak, he said, "Your friends Dilip. Aaziz and Pronoy told me about the matter and they called the Police."

On Sunday, in the evening, it was the last day and the next Monday they all will go for the Durga puja holidays in their homes. Debarun was walking in the road side of his university suddenly a wind passed from his face it was a overcast day and very windy, he saw Natasha came towards him, he said, "you are here." Natasha said nothing she just smiled and kissed him, at that moment his mobile rang, it was the call from his home, that he was selected for the job as a Civil service officer for the state government of Tripura and he have to join after the puja vacation in his home town Tripura. Debarun understood that it was his illusion that he saw Natasha and also he understood he has to leave the University now his all friends and all who all helped him so much. Suddenly the rain started, he went to his hostel, but he was unable to reach his hostel because there were heavy showers of rain with thunderstorms. One of his friend called him and said him to come inthe bus stand with was located in the University campus. Debarun came and sat next to her, her name was Nabamallika she was an Assamese girl from Jorhat, she was from the Economics department and used to come to his department to study Sociology because they was having a elective paper of Sociology Nabamallika was the girl whom he used to love during his Masters sessions in the University, when she comes in front to him his heart starts pounding, and now she was doing her M Phil course. Nabamallika said, "So you are leaving on Monday." Debarun said, "Monday yes, thats tomorrow" Nabamallika said, "You will be back after 15 days." Debarun said, "I will not come back." Nabamallika said, "Why?" Debarun said, "I got a job." Nabamallika said, "That great what job?" Debarun said, "Job in Civil service of the state goverment of Tripura." Nabamallika said, "Great you should give a party." Debarun said. "Yes I am giving a chicken party tonight in the hostel but you cannot come there." Nabamallika said, "I know next day all of them will miss you so much." Debarun said, "And you will not miss me." Nabamallika smiled and said, "Some questions do not have any answer." Debarun said, "I think I got my answer." Nabamallika said, "I am getting married Debarun the next month and I will leave this place." Debarun said, "Congrats, what a good news we should celebrate together." Nabamallika kept quiet and did not say anything Debarun said, "what about your studies." Nabamallika said, "1 month is left to complete my M.Phil, my marriage will be after 15 days during the Durga puja holidays, I will come and complete my course and I will leave the University." Debarun said, "the rain has stopped I have to leave now or it will start again Nabamallika said, "I will miss you Debarun." Debarun looked back at her and said, "I knew that, good bye." Debarun went to his hostel.

3

Arun's Silence

Later he would tell his story to him. It all started in the year 2011 in the month of September. Arun Sen came from Tripura to study his Masters course in Assam University: Silchar. The day was a rainy one when he entered the hostel, after a long summer vacation from his hometown. He kept shut his mouth and was sitting in the bed in the room with his roommate, Paul Das was from Assam. It was 10 pm, their dinner was over. Arun went to his room and was lying in the bed and reading a book, Taiwan came towards Arun and said, "Do you have exam tomorrow." Arun said, "No, just reading a story book. "Taiwan said, "I think you are reading karma sutra."Arun said, "Shut up, go to your room Taiwan." Paul said, "Arun da why you are not saying anything after you came from the vacation the last one year you used to make a lot of fun what has happened to you are you alright." Arun did not say anything but just smiled. Taiwan was from Manipur, he also talks very much, and he said. "Arun you want to study."

Arun said, "No I just want to take some rest. Paul said, "Alright Arun da you are very tired today you take rest I and Taiwan da is also feeling very sleepy, good night." Arun said, good night."

Arun woke up in the morning and went to attend his class. Arun is very quiet he does not talk much he always remains very silent. Nasrim said, "Arun I think you will attend the lecture of Professor Sharma." Arun said, "Yes I will attend, but that is after 1 hour it will take time."Nasrim said, "Then where are you going now." Arun said. "To the canteen to drink a cup of tea, do you want to come with me."Nasrim said, "Alright lets go" In the canteen. Nasrim said, "Arun why you are so quiet" Arun said, "What quiet." Nasrim said, "We all friends want to talk with you but it seems that you want to avoid us." Arun said, "No it is not that I just want to remain busy with myself." Nasrim said. "If you have any problem thenplease tell me why you are so upset after coming from the vacation." Arun said, "No, nothing happened to me; let's go, it's time for the class."

The class had started Professor Sharma entered the class and started to deliver his lecture. Professor Sharma said. "Today's lecture topic is taboo." The class started, Arun was feeling very depressed and came out of the class, looking at him all his friends had a question in their minds what had happened to him. Arun came out of the class and went to his hostel, the hostel was empty nobody was there because all the students went to attend their classes. He opened the door of his room kept his bag on the table and lay down in the bed and started to think something, but what the matter really was, hidden in him he did not want to say anything to anyone but kept it within himself.

At 6 pm in the hostel, a boy knocked the door of Arun s room. Arun opened the door and said, "Rajiv you are here what happened?." Rajiv said, "Arun da Paul and Taiwan are not here." Arun said. "No, they did not come why anything important?" Rajiv said, "The warden called for a meeting at 7:30 pm please tell them and if I meet them I will tell." Arun said, "Ok I will be there in the meeting." Rajiv said, "Ok, warden was asking about you."Arun said, "Why." Rajiv said, "I do not know." Arun said, "I will meet him in the meeting."

It was 6 pm all the students had gathered in the hall for the meeting which took place in the common room of the hostel. Arun was absent in the meeting. The warden said, "Where is Arun I want to discuss the sports equipments that he has to bring, he did not gave me any application." Rajiv said, "Sir, I told him there is a meeting." Warden said, 'If he is in the room go and call him." Paul said, "Sir there is no need to call him, he is not there when I came I saw him leaving the hostel, I think he was going somewhere." Warden said, "Do as I say Paul, you just call him in his mobile." Paul said, "I have been trying sir, but the mobile is switched off." Warden said, "What could happen to him? You do one thing Paul when he will come to the hostel you or any one of you meet him tell him to meet me, he is the sportssecretary of the hostel but doesn't have any responsibility tell him to meet me immediately when he comes. "It was 9 pm Arun came to the hostel. and went to his rooms, Paul said, "Where were you? You were not present in the meeting" Arun said, "I went to the health centre I am suffering a little problem of throat pain." Paul said, "Warden asked me to tell you when you will arrive you should go and meet him."Arun said, "Ok, I am going to meet him" Paul said, "He is very angry with you, you go and meet him as soon as possible" Arun said, "Okay."

Arun went to meet his warden, his warden used to stay in the ground floor of the hostel his name was

Dr Deepak Sen he was a Professor of Psychology department of the Univenity. He used to live in the hotel with other students. Arun entered the room, Deepak said. "Arun come in sit here, just let me wash my hands I had my dimer just now Deepak went to wash his hands, It was a cold windy night, December mood in the mid September, he was looking out the window to the drops of rain that were falling on the glasses, and the street fight featuring the drops of rain Deepak came and sat behind Arun and said, "Arun what had happened to you? Why you were not present in the meeting? Arun said. "Sir, I was in the health centre I brought t medicines for me, I am suffering from throat pain" Deepak said, "You should have told me carlier, I told you to meet me before the meeting but you did not come." Arun said, "I am sorry Sir." Deepak said, "ok, did you make any application for the sports equipments." Anun said, "Yes sir, I have made, here it is Deepak said, "Ok, give me."Arun said, "Sir, may I leave now" Deepak said, "You had your dinner" Arun said, "Yes just now." Deepak said, "Do you have any exam tomorrow." Arun said, "No Sir" Deepak said. "You please sit here I need to talk with you." Arun said, "Yes sir." Deepak said, "Arun I heard some news about you" Arun said, "I did anything wrong sir." Deepak said, "No no, you did nothing, but it seems to me you are very silent now a days, from your department your professor said that you are not attending the classes and they are not getting any good performance which they used to get earlier, What is the reasonArun that made you silent. "Arun said. "no reason sir. "Deepak said, "Arun I am a professor of psychology I come with many patients I am not a teacher only but also a doctor. If you have any problem you can tell me, is there any problem in the hostel did Aziz locked the door when you were in your room which he did last month? I still remember that it was 2 am late night you were sleeping you called me in my mobile and I said the security to open the door, did anything happened liked that or it something else." Arun raised his voice and said, "Sir nothing I do not know why all are asking me the same question, what is the matter with them all. I am totally unaware what the fuck is that it is none of any one business with my life." Deepak was quiet he did not said anything but he understood there was something in his mind."

Arun bit his lips and felt helpless annoyance rising up within him as he thought back to that conversation. He had allowed himself to be taken unaware by the sonorous, confident voice at the other end, and for no reason what so ever. Quite soberly, he could still have said no. But he had missed the crucial moment, the moment it could be so natural to say, it could be a misunderstanding. Arun said, "I am sorry sir, I could not mean in that way" Deepak said, "I understand Arun there is something wrong with you I am of 60 years and I can feel the worries going through your mind, I understand you are very worried for something if you want to share with me no problem I am not only your teacher but also a friend of yours I think you are very tired you go and take rest." Arun said, "How I can take rest sir? When I close my eyes the incidents penetrate like a dark shadow." Deepak said, "What incidents please tell me." Arun said, "Yes sir, I will tell you because it is disturbing me all the time in each and every moment."

Deepak said, "Tell me what happened." Arun said. "It was started in the summer vacation when I went to my home town in Tripura, some of my friends told me to go to silchar again for a picnic." Deepak said, "For a picnic but you left silchar and went to your home, your friends were fromthis hostel." Arun said. "No sir, they were from department of Social Anthropology Deepak said, "I see, after then you came to silchar." Arun said, "Yes I had to come because they were my close friends and they organized the picnic especially for me." Deepak said. "After that what happened?" Arun said, "We all had a lot of fun there in the picnic spot near the airport area, the area was surrounded by hills and rivers it wasnice and a pleasant "Deepak said, "After that you went to your home." Arun said, "No I wanted to go to my home but my friends planned to visit Kolkata." Deepak said, "Kolkata for what purpose." Arun said, "My cousin brothers marriage was there and I had to go to Kolkata, my parents went there very early and they called me to come to Kolkata from Silchar by air, I reached the air port and sat in the plane, the plane started I wanted to go to the bathroom as I got up from my seat there was a jerking of the plane and by chance I fell upon an airhostess." Deepak smiled and said, "Ok its interesting tell me the story." Arun said. "When I got up one of my shirt buttons was stuck on the uniform button of her I tried to get rid of it and also she was doing the same thing everyone was looking at us I was feeling very embarrassed at that moment, but she was totally normal there was no anxiety in her eyes she opened the tangle and smiled" Deepak said, "So what happened further."Arun said, "I met her in the airport in Kolkata when the flight landed. I asked her name she said her name was Trisha we both became good friends and used to spend time together in the park street area I can't say when I fell in love with her with a beautiful airhostess it was courageous on my part but also not normal to my part. One day I shared my feeling with her she smiled, and she told me she also had fallen in love with me the day when my shirt button got stuck in her uniform button. One day both of us were walking through the road of park street it was 7 pm, suddenly it began to rain both of us went to a nearby hotel and took shelter in a room I am a student I was having no money she said she would pay and there was no need to worry she was younger than me she joined the airhostess academy when she passed her class 12" exams. We both entered the room and locked the room. "Arun stopped atthat moment, Deepak said, "Tell me the story I want to listen." Arun said, "No sir. I can't say what happened next." Deepak said. "Do you accept me as your friend." Arun said, "Yes but sir."Deepak said. "Then tell everything."Arun said, "Ok sir listen, she was completely wet, she wanted to change her dress and went to the changing room and changed her clothes, she came out of the room wearing a erotic dress a surge of erotic feeling overtook me, that put my pants bulged up.She laid down on her knees touched my penis opened my pant and she was playing with my penis and it became much harder, she put her mouth in it and started giving me a blowjob,I was feeling hornythat I was in a deep pleasure, she told me she want to taste my cum as much as she can,I came closer to her, gripped her back and pulled her towards me, now I could feel her cleavages by my whole body; what a feeling was that which turns out all the pleasures in the world. I kissed her, she kissed me I came closer to her slipped my hand over her breast cupped them, caressed and brought her closer to me, undressed her kissed on her navel, slowly my hands explored her whole body which made her shiver with pleasure.At that moment I wanted to go deep, but she stopped me but I cannot stop myself. She lay on the bed after some moments she turned and told me to fuck her from the back: it was the perfect doggy position, it was our experience of watching many porn movies; she knew all the porn moves, soon after she expertly executed the reverse, and she told me to cum on her, and that brought the juice out of me. We were exhausted with pleasure. It was not that which I really wanted, but, it happened why? The question even now singes my mind." Deepak said, "Your love for her had crossed the social boundaries. "Arun said, "I am sorry sir I cannot explain how it happened."

Deepak said, "it happened because both of you were in the stage of sub conscious instinct, tell me what happened after that night." Arun said. "everything was normal, we meet with each other, one day she told me tonight she has to go for a marriage party. I said I also had an invitation for my brother marriage for that I came here in Kolkata, that evening I went to that marriage I had a lot of fun suddenly I met Trisha in that marriage also I met with her parents my family members came when they saw her parents then I asked my uncle, do you know her? My uncle said. "yes, she is the cousin daughter of your father's sister." Deepak was stunned and said, "What are you talking about, it is true, she is your sister." Arun said. "Yes, She was my sister." Deepak said, "shocked to hear the truth how can it be? How can?"

Deepak said, "After that what happened." Arun said. "5 days I did not meet her no phone call nothing not even she did not received my calls she was staying in Kolkata and it was the time for me to leave Kolkata and to go to Tripura, I went to her house her mother said she was not well she was sick I do not know what was her condition I was in need to talk with her but I could not, a question in my mind gnawed at me how could I face her and it was the same with her."

Deepak said, "Yeah its true, you did not meet her before you left Kolkata." Arun said, "One day she was in the balcony of her flat all alone I went there touched her shoulder she cried and hugged me she said she could not face the situation even she could not sleep in the night when she closed her eyes she saw the intimate moments between us, she felt she was pregnant she said she could not erase the past no matter how much I wanted to, I said her we could make things all right, she said every time she looked at me it hurts, and she was the one who had to decide the right thing I asked her what she would do, she told, she will do what is right for both of us, she smiled and slowly went near the balcony and jumped from there and died, now I cannot sleep in the nightI can still feel her presence her face haunts me like a nightmare tell me sir what I can do I am the reason for her death each and every moment I curse myself for that reason." Deepak was silent for a moment, and said, "Arun do not cry son, it was not your fault it was the time, time plays a unpredictable role in our life, its 11 pm go and sleep now you are very tired take rest." Arun went to his room and got up in the bed. Paul said, "You are so late? Had he scolded you or said something wrong is you alright?" Arun said, "Yes Paul, things may be alright or may not be in any time." Paul said, "I did not understand what you said." Arun said, "Nothing, good night Paul." Paul said, "good night."

Next Morning, Arun did not go to his department to attend his regular classes. He was sitting in his room and after few minutes he went out of his hostel playground which was in front of his hostel and sat in the stairs of the ground, it was 2 pm Deepak came to the hostel to have his lunch, he saw Arun from the window he came toward Arun and sat nextto him, and said, "It's quite cold today, last night heavy shower made the weather quite cold, you did not go to attend your classes." Arun said, "No sir, I am not feeling well today." Deepak said, "For how many days you will do like this? You have semester after two months." Arun said, "Sir, I want to be alone."Deepak said, "Arun we live alone, we die alone, and everything is just an illusion."Arun said, "I am scared Sir." Deepak said, "May be you are too scared that someone might actually want to be with you." Arun was silent. Deepak said, "Listen Arun I can't say whhat Trisha did was right for her but I know she did have no choice she loved you and for that she made this choice." Arun said, "It was her choice, toleave me with unbearable burden of guilt for my whole life." Deepak said, "Arun she was right when she said you can't erase the past, no matter how hard you want to, so she made this choose, we all make choices the hard part is living with them." Arun said, "Yes sir may be you are right." Deepak said, "I am getting retired after 2 year and you are also leaving after 1 year, you can't erase the past but you can live in the present, take it as a gift, live it, come I will drop you to your department get in my car." Arun said, "Sir it's already 2.30 pm." Deepak said, "So what the lunch break is over you have two more classes after the lunch break." Arun said, "Yes, sir I have but it is late now." Deepak said, "nothing is late go to your hostel come get ready within 5 minutes I am waiting for you" Arun said, "Yes sir." Arun went to the hostel dressed up and went to attend his classes. When he enters his department one of his junior named Abbas said, "Arun da you are looking quite fresh today." Arun said, "I made my choice to look forward but sometimes, we make choices and the hard part is living with them." Abbas said, "I did not understand Dada." Arun said, "No nothing my class has started." Abbas said, "Ok Arun da will talk with you later my class is also started." On the way to the class he slipped and fall. After he had brushed the dirt's from his shirt, he stood for a moment and closed his eyes. He thought about the sounds ticking on the wall clock of his department he stepped slowly.

Arun said to himself nothing had happened, he entered his class.

4

Sam Are You There

The morning was chili, it was nearly 7.30 am. Dev wake up very early, but, not too early it was the time for him to go to the ground to play his cricket match which was organized between the hostels of Assam University, Silchar,the year 2006. Birancy knocking at the door calling Dev. "Oii get up, it's time for the match, why are you sleeping till now, what happened?" Dev opened the door and said, "Come inside, just wait I am wearing my jersey, last night I had a late sleep for that reason I am late to get up early "Birancy said, "Why last night you were watching porn." Dev said, "yeah your girl friend's porn. "Birancy said. "Ha ha, alright get ready I am waiting for you." Dev said, "sit, I am ready we will go together. "The match began, David said, "Dev please entertain us." Dev said, "look what the fuck I will play today." Dev hitted 3 sixes in 3 deliveries, Mukunda shouted and said, "Dev da khub bhalo khalcho".

The Match got over and they won the match. After a minute all of them went to the dining hall to take their breakfast and to go to their respected departments. In the dining hall David said Dev, "Hey Dev did you done the assignment regarding the fiction writing on ancient European literature our Professor Rajesh Mohanta gave you."Dev said, "Yes, but let's see whether he accepts my work or not". Dunhill said, "Dev you know one of a professor in my Department Biology says, to control the population we should use condom." Everyone laughed in the dining hall and Jamie said, "I think he is very much experienced in that, he might have been a perfect sexologist." David said, "Now a day's Jamie is leaning many bad things I think Dev taught him." Jamie said, "Yes I am doing PhD under Dev da." David said, "In which subject." Jamie said, "Sexology in free society." Dev said, "Just stop this non sense, or I will kick you outfrom here." Jamie said, "Oak, sorry please do not be angry I was just joking, let's go to our departments." David said, "ok, let's move to our departments."

Dev was studying English in Assam University. The University was located near the border of Assam and Mizoram. He was staying in the hostel. The hostel was surrounded by big trees and hills and there is only forests which is been seen at that place, but, he sometimes passes his time sitting in the window side and looking at the Bhuban hills. It can be said that the hostel was surrounded by forests and for that reason the local people staying there had seen leopards many times especially in the month of September to October. So it had been said to all the boys of this hostel not to move in the night outside the hostel campus.

Dev went to his department and one of his friends named Nazima said, "Dev had you finished your assignment today you have to present first." Dev said, "Yeah, I know that and after that yours." Nazima said, "Yes, so all the best." Rupali said, "How are you Dev come sit with me today." Dev said, "Thanks Rupali today you are looking very beautiful." Rupali said, "Thanks so sweet of you." Dev said, "where is yours friends Debolena, Anita, Dippaneta and Swarnali." Rupali said, "they are all sitting at the next row they are very angry with you, your new rivals."

Parbin said, "Dev see our respected teacher is coming, he is so rough in his behavior." Nasrim said, "Yes, today let's see what he does to our assignment." Dev said. "Yes, I can't say what will happen to me."

Professor Rajesh entered the classroom, everybody was very nervous, when he entered the class with a person so everyone got nervous as well as surprised and say to one another who is the man came with him.

Professor Rajesh said, "good morning student here my friend Remit kalita came from Jorhat University a renowned professor of Assamese literature, he will address you all today and I and he will check your assignments. You all please come one by one." Professor Rajesh had issues with Dev, both of the professors started checking the assignments. Now the turn of Dev. Dev gave his assignment to Professor Rajesh. Professor Rajesh did not look in his assignment and said, "By one look of mine I can say that your assignment is totally hopeless as you." Dev said, "What the hopeless I wrote Sir, without reading my work how can you say so?" Professor Rajesh said, "see your words everything you wrote wrong there is no match with one sentence with the other sentence." Professor Remit Kalita said, "The condition is the same as when this Bengali people placed their language replacing our Assamese language."

Dev became very angry, and he did not know what he should say this people are bringing the historical conflicts in between his assignment. Dev said, "Why are you saying so? It is an assignment and sir you are bringing the history of Barak Valley language movement, that's means you are bringing the communal riots even now, that you brought on 19 May 1969, in Cachar district of Assam. "Professor Rajesh said. "Mind your language, are you challenging us. Mr. Dev I will expel you." Dev said, "I know sir but it does not mean to be expelled by you because I do not care you are bringing our culture and language in the way, you are totally wrong our language does not replaced your language it's yours language replaced our language." Both the professors got angry and Professor Remit said, "Shut up what you know do you have the guts to say anything, say." Dev said, "11 people was killed by the Assamese police In April, 1960, a proposal was raised at the Assam Pradesh Congress Committee, to declare Assamese as the one and only official language of the state settlements. The violence reached its peak between July and September, during which an estimated 50,000 Bengali Hindus fled the Brahmaputra valley and arrived in West Bengal Another 90,000 fled to Barak valley and other regions of the North East,4,019 huts and 58houses belonging to Bengali Hindus were vandalized and destroyed in 25 villages of Goreswar in Kamrup district, which was the worst affected by violence. Nine Bengali Hindus were killed and more than one hundred injure." Professor Remit said, "get out of the class and also you are not allowed to participate in the seminar to present your paper on fictional poetry writing which will take place and know one thing if you do not present your paper you are not allowed to sit for the examination now leave my class" Dev said, "Yeah, I get out."

Dev want outside of the department in a harsh way. He was on his way to his hostel he got a call from his mother saying how are you have you submitted your assignment. Dev told he will submit but they refused to accept it.After few minutes his father called him and was asking about the assignment, he said he submitted but got rejected and both of his parents was very worried and told no problem that's need some improvement of his work and to submit it latter.

It was a cold night of December and the narrow roads of the Durgaquna,Silcharwas quite and silent Dev was moving to his hostel it was nearly 8.00 pm and his friend Birancy called him in his mobile saying where he is and he said coming to the hostel. Nothing could be seen because of the mist, and the cold wind blowing making the atmosphere with shivering stocks. It was dark and Dev could hear the groaning of pines, it is to be said not to walk in the streets at night because of Leopards' seen by the local people, which used to come in this months of September to December. In the local villages it is also to be seen and it had attacked many people in the villages. Suddenly there was a sound of the leopard moving around he then run to go to the university and could not, two of the leopards came to him Dev was very frightened and do not know what to do, at that time a man came with a gun and shoot the leopard in its leg an both of the leopard run away. Dev was looking at the man, a tall man having a stout body with white bears in his face. He said. "What your name is and what you are doing here right now?"Dev said. "Myname is Dev Roy I am a student at the university, I was going to the hostel" The man said. "My name is Sam Bhattacharya, you do not know it is not the right time to walk in this place." Dev said, "No I just went to the market." Sam said, "Stop come to my house stay here tonight go the hostel next morning" Dev said, "no need I heard about you my friends say that you stay here for a long time you are a alcoholic and speaks total nonsense, thanks for saving me I want to leave." Sam said, "I know that, the leopards are roaming here I will not come again to save you, they will eat you up as their dinner."Dev had no choice but to go Sam's house and stay there for a night.

When Dev entered his house he saw that there are lot of books, the whole house is surrounded by books and notes it was a small bungalow can be said as home of books. Dev asked him, "You live here alone." Sam said, "its night eat this chapattis and some a bit of vegetables I do not know an Unknown guest will come in home today." Nextmorning. Sam said, "Dev woke up man, it's already 7 pm." Devwoke up in hesitation and said, "I have to leave right now I have a class at 10 am." Sam said. it not too late come I have prepared a special breakfast for you have a cup of coffee, oak do you like egg plough Dev said." I love but with 2 pieces of boiled egg. "Dev took his breakfast and was on his way to the university hostel, at that moment when he was leaving the house of Sam, Sam said, "Dev just a moment I saw some of you writing in your note book. "Dev said, "You opened my bag. how can you do that." Sam said, "I did so because your bag was torn and I stitched it up." Dev said, "I am sorry" Sam said. "You should be, so I found that there are some forms of mistakes in your sentence construction and prepositions you need some improvement." Dev said, "you are saying in such a way that you are a great scholar of English literature." Sam said, "If you need help you can come in my house any time, go to your class or you will be late."

Dev went to his university hostel and was got ready to go to his class Birancy said, "Hey where were you last night, we all were worried for you." Dev said, "One of my uncle house." Utpal said, "I thought with that girl Dev." Dev said, "what you thing you thing ass hole like yourself fuck your thoughts." Utpal said, "Just joking man." David said, "Come Dev lets go to our department, one thing I want to tell you that Professor Juliasen wants to meet you". Dev said. "Concerning". David said, "I do not know, I think regarding the internal exams which you gave last month." There was a discussion going on the hostel. Dev hostel boarders were all little bit strange in their characters. There were different groups of people, starting from tribals and non- tribal's, such as Boros, Mishing and Biharies, Uttar Pradesh and Assamese as well as Bengali. But there was only five Bengali boys the names; Panna, Pronoy, Utpal, Saurav and Dev. Birancy was Assamese he was the best friend of Dev followed by Panna and Pronoy, both of them were junior to Dev, and both of them were Bengalis.

The Assamese and the Biharieshave a conflict among each other. The Assamese doesn't involve themselves in the need of the Biharies and the Bihariesdoes not involve themselves in the need of the Assameses, both of the group remains excluded among each other. The hostel was a bit peculiar in its type, it was situated in the beneath of the university campus which make the hosteller different to go and enter the hostel in time. The hostel was very much famous for its violent act drinking alcohol and smoking was a famous scenario of the hostel, followed by watching pornography like T.V Shows in most of the rooms.

In the department. Dev went to meet Julia sen, she was the assistant Professor of the department, and Dev went to Prof Julia sen in her room. Dev said. "Madam, may I come in?" Prof Julia said, "yes, come Dev sit, I was going through your assignment I found that the things which you wrote is just the same in the materials in the books, you had just copied, you should understand and write the situation. I even saw your answer you only just mug up and write it, it's too good to do it in a very easy way but it will not help you in your every steps of your life." Dev said, "What should I do now?" Prof Julia said, "your words are not up to the mark you just repeat you assignment again, I am giving you your assignment and giving you a week, finish your assignment and return to me the next week." Dev said, "But how can I finished it in a week."Prof Julia said, "I am giving you 10 days my dear I do not give so much time to any other students, do it, and see I will talk to Professor Rajesh for you to participate in the seminar, let's see what he says" Dev said," "Ok, I will try my best, thank you Madam."

Dev went out of the room and attend his class. In the class Dev was thinking about his assign ment how he would finish it in such a short time. At that moment Hasina one friend of Dev said. "Dev what happen do not worry you will complete your work do not worry." Dev said, "Hope so." Hasina said. "I will talk to you after the class gets over." Dev said, "Alright."

After the class, Dev went out to have launch in the backyard of his department hostel, "here comes Hasina," said Dev from his mind. Hasina said, "Dev come lets have lunch together." Dev said, "Ok." At that moment Rupali and Nazima came towards them and they said, they want to join them in lunch.

In the canteen, four of them were sitting together and talking about them, Hasina said,"Dev you remember that girl Navanita Mahanta, whom you liked so much." Dev said, "one day I saw her in her transparent sari she was looking so beautiful." Hasina said, "She is an Assamese girl and Assamese and Bengalis does not match well." Rupali said. "Yes, I agree with Hasina it's true."

Dev said, "We all remember the Barak Valley Movement, is not we." Nazima said, "Dev let's talk about something. I heard one night you were in an old man's house which is located in that hill region; I heard that old man is little bit strange." Dev said. "He is fully strange. I was in danger he saved me, I cannot say about him leave him, the lunch time is over lets go to our classes."

After his classes got over, he went to his hostel and started preparing his lessons for the assignment. But nothing is coming in his mind; he was feeling very sleepy and went to sleep. Next morning he woke up early and went to Sam's house, he has no choice but to do so, he does not know what Sam's know or not but he want some help of someone, there was no person who can help him, so he does not have any choice, he went to Sam.

Dev was knocking at the Sams door. Sam opened the door and said, "I knew you will come it's nice to see you "Dev said, "I did not wanted to come here but I have no choice." Sam said, "But I think you made the right choice." Dev said, "I have to complete my assignment, but I did not brought any book you see to it " Sam said. "Show me your assignment". Dev opened his bag and shown him the assign meant and said. "Here it is, I think it is a very easy task for you, and a difficult task for me."

Sam was reading the assignment and Dev was sitting with him. Sam said, "this assignment is not so difficult, its need a description and also a evaluation of the European theories of literature. You should know to put the adjective and verb in the proper place." Dev was surprised thinking that how this man knows so much about it, his knowledge is much vast then the Universities Professor. Dev said, "How do you know so much." Sam said, "it s none of your business, do your own work, now write this passage I am giving you for your assignment after that I will give you another." Dev said. "My writing is over." Sam said, "Good, now write as I wrote about 4000 words." Dev said, "How I can do so are you crazy, I have to attend my class today in the evening." Sam said. "Do you have an exam." Dev said, "No" Sam said, "Than do it, not need to attend the class". Dev said, "But how could I write this about 4000 words in an hour." Sam said, "Than get the fuck out of my house right now, and submit nothing to your teacher, and when your teacher will say about your assignment than say what the fuck you wrote." Dev was nervous he can't say anything but did what Sam told him to do.

After 1 hour he finished his work and said, "Sam I did it, its took a lot of time." Sam, said, "good, I wanted that the thing is that you should keep patience in yourself which you does not have, never trust yourself now what you did you show me." Dev shown him the work, Sam was evaluating it, Sam said, "Now go and show to it to your teacher tomorrow." Dev said, "Let me leave now." Sam said, "Wait, have launch and leave." Dev took his lunch and went to his hostel. Next morning he went to his department, to his Assistant Professor Julia sen with his assignment. Dev said. "Madam, may I come in." Julia sen said, "Please come in Dev." Dev entered his room. Julia said, "So how are you? Did you finish your assignment?" Dev said, "Yes, Madam." Julia said, "Then show me." Dev opened his bag and took out the copy of his work." Julia sen was looking in his assignment and said, "it is perfect you wrote it." Dev said, "Yes." Julia Sen said, "your words have improved a lot you are almost perfect in few days, very good keep this spirit." Dev said, "Madam may I leave." Julia sen said, "Sit why you are always in such a hurry." Dev said, "I have to go somewhere." Julia sen said, "alright I will show your assignment to Professor Rajesh let's see what he says." Dev said, "alright, bye madam."

Dev came out of his department with a very happy face. He straight went to Sam house, he knocked in Sam house. Sam opened the door and said, "Come I was waiting for you." Dev came inside, Sam said. "So what your professor said about your assignment." Dev said, "She said it was an excellent work." Sam smiled and said, "I knew that." Dev said. "Can I ask you a question Sam?"

Sam said. "Yes what." Dev said, "How do you know so much?" Sam smiled and said nothing. Dev was moving his eyes in the room and saw many books of Sam he had also seen it earlier when he fast came here but today he saw a metal plate like a thing, he went to that and found it was made of metal. Dev said. "Sam this price looks like a Novel prize I know it is not that ok, from where you brought that." Sam said. "It's a novel prize." Dev said. "Are you joking" Sam said, "No I am not." Devsaid, "Are you crazy." Sam said. "I am not, it's the novel prizefor literature in 1975." Dev was surprised and was thinking what the fucking bullshit the old man is talking about. Dev said, "Novel Prize for literature was given to Professor Samal Bhattacharya in short Sam in 1975 after that no one found him he is still a questions in every bodies mind, he graduated from Oxford University and one day he ran away and no idea where he is now I read about you in my school even our professors tells us about your works in the origin of English literature, Are you that man." Sam said. "Yes I am that man." Dev said," then why are you hiding like that are you crazy if anyone know you are staying here, all will come to meet you even the President or the Prime Minister of this country." Sam said. "You will not tell anyone about me." Dev said, "Why are you doing so are you drunk again and speaking so harsh, I heard that your wife left you for that reason." Sam got angry and shouted and said. "Shut up, what the hell you are talking about me, get the fuck out of my house and do not come here any time, go away." Dev said, "all right I go away. good bye."

Dev went out from his house, Sam on the other side thinking the he should not be so rude to him, he is young and innocent there is something wrong between both of them. Dev went to his hostel and was thinking that Sam what is the matter with him why he was hiding himself from the world.

The next morning Dev woke up early. He went to his department to attain his classes and was coming back to his hostel. In his way to the hostel he saw Sam was waiting for him, he was surprised to see him. He said "Sam what are you doing her?." Sam said, "Just waiting for you." Dev said. "Please do not stand here you know my friends may come any time and say I am talking with an alcoholic beast." Sam said, "I heard that your hostel borders are also drunk every time."

Dev said. "Let me leave I do not want to talk more." Sam said, "Dev do not be angry with me I am sorry for the last day what I said you." Dev said, "I am also sorry I would not said so what I wanted to say." Sam said, "Then please come with me out of the university near the lake side." Dev said, "No, I have to play a match." Sam said, "I know I saw you playing cricket I like your game you play very well, but I request you to come with me and have a walk near the lake side, or I will think that you are angry with me."

Dev went with Sam outside the University campus for a walk. Dev and Sam was walking near the lake both of them was confused what they should say to each other. Sam said, "I know what you said me last day. You were right, you are a tuff kid and nobody could understand the depth of you." Dev said. "I apologize for what I said." Sam said, "No you are not Sorry for that reason, you know I wrote a lot of books won the novel prize having 25 years spending in the university of oxford teaching the students, the scholars, if I ask you about Shakespeare you can say very easily who was he, works ofMichael Foucault, The history of sexuality, if I ask you about women, you'd probably give me a syllabus about your personal favourites. You may have even been laid a few times. But you can't tell me what it feels like to wake up next to a woman and feel truly happy. You're a tough kid. And I'd ask you about war, the time when in Cachar district was going through a violent situation the conflict between Bengali and the Assamese I and my wife Rita went to England, and settled there forever. You've never held your best friend's head in your lap, watch him gasp his last breath looking to you for help. I'd ask you about love, you'd probably quote me a sonnet. Known someone? That could level you with her eyes, feeling like God put an angel on earth just for you. Who could rescue you from the depths of hell? And you wouldn't know what it's like to be her angel, to have that love forher, is there forever, through anything, through cancer. And you wouldn't know about sleeping sitting up in the hospital room for two months, holding her hand, because the doctors could see in your eyes that the terms "visiting hours" don't apply to you. You don't know about real loss, 'cause it only occurs when you've loved something more than you love yourself. Rita was suffering from cancer and it caused her to dead. It is not that what we think is right it is that are we right to think about others."

Dev kept silent for a moment. Sam said, "It's getting dark now lets go to my house, do you want to stay in my house tonight." Dev said, "No the warden said nobody can leave the hostel without an application, but, I will come tomorrow." Sam said, "Alright."

From that day both of them became best friends Dev every time visit to Sam house, Sam helps him in his studies and help him in writing skills. In Sam's house, Dev said, "Sam I think I should write a book." Sam said, "Why?" Dev said, "One of my friends said if you write a book than a girl will sleep with you." Sam said, "A girl will sleep with you if you write a bad book." Dev said, "Very funny, by the way what are you reading." Sam said, "Folktales of the missing tribe of Arunachal Pradesh." Dev said, "This tribe is from Assam I have a friend among this tribe." Sam said, "May be, but this group of people came from Tibet many years ago for food and survival and came to Arunachal started agriculture and after that a large portion of them migrated to Assam." Dev said, "It's a very new thing for me to know." Sam said, "Another thing do you know about the Assamese people." Dev said, "What?" Sam said, "Very interesting this people of Assam are not actually Hindus." Dev said, "Then who're they?" Sam said, "This people are Thai in its origin migrated from Thailand thousand years back and came to the north east region of India and named the place Assam." Dev said, "Very interesting Sam. How do you know so much?" Sam said, "What?" Dev said, "Sorry you are a Professor you will know much more than the others." Sam said, "Do you know about the Assamese language." Dev said, "What?" Sam said, "Do you find any similarity between this Assamese language and Bengali language." Dev said, "Yes, there are some words which are very similar with Bengali." Sam said, "It's because the Assamese language is taken from the Bengali and Sanskrit manuscript." Dev said, "You are a genius Sam but why are you hiding yourself." Sam said, "You know that very well about me, can I ask you for a promise." Dev said, "What?" Sam said, "I will help you to improve you assignment and your words and your studies, but, do not say anything about me to anyone." Dev said, "Ok, Sam I will never say it to any one, about you." Sam said. "Dev you are from Tripura." Dev said. "Yes, I am." Sam said. "Did you read any folktales fromTripura." Dev said, "No I did not have anything." Sam said, "oak forget about the folktales you know the story of Ramayana and the Mahabharata." Dev said, "Yes I know." Sam said, "Who is your favourite character in Mahabharata." Dev said, "Karna." Sam said. "The same as mine, can you name the bow which was given to karna by his teacher Lord Parashuram." Dev said. "Yes the Vijay Dhanush, it was the dhanush of Parashurama and it brings victory to the warrior." Sam said, "the question is that you know who made this bow and for whom." Dev said, "No I did not know that can you say." Sam said. "This bow was made by Bishwakarma god for Lord Shiva to destroy the state of Tripura." Dev said. "Tripurawhy?" Sam said, "Because Tripura was made by the sons of Tarakasura and Lord Shiva destroyed it. After that Lord Shiva gave this Vijay bow to his student Lord Parashuram and than Lord Parashuram gave it to his student Karna." Dev said. "Today I came to know many things but now I have to leave. Good bye."

Dev went to his hostel. Pronoy was knocking at his door and was saying, "Dev da is you there?" Dev said, "yeah, wait I am opening the door."Pronoy came inside, Pronoy said, "are you sleeping." Dev said, "No, justsitting and writing notes." Pronoy said, "Actually today afternoon I sawyou near that old man's house what you were doing there." Dev said, "Nothing,just a visit." Pronoy said, "He is not so good." Dev said, "Whatever heis, he is my teacher, please do not say anything about him." Pronoy said, "I was not saying that the rest of the boys were saying even the hostelwarder he wants to meet you tomorrow morning." Dev said, "Why."Pronoy said, "no idea, ok let me leave now I am feeling sleepy." Devsaid, "Ok, I am also feeling very sleepy good night."

Next morning Dev woke up and went to his hostel warden room, which was in the ground floor of the building. Dev knocked at the door and the door was opened by the warden his name was Abhi Bishwas.Dev said,"Sir you called me." Abhi Bishwas said, "Yes, I was going through the attendance list of the hostel I found that your name is missing." Dev said, "Yes Sir, sometimes I stay in my uncle's house." Abhi said, "Uncle who to your uncle I did not heard anything about that, you are trying to fool me."Dev said, "Why should I fool you?" Abhi said, "Dev I can' allow you to go there and stay for a long time outside the university campus at night without an application, and you know now a days a communal riot going in the town of Silchar so I did not allow any student from the hostel to go to the town for their personal needs, I do not want to take any risk, and do you see there is a continuous police protection in the university isdue to the problem of that town between the Assamese and Boro people." Dev said, "Sir, it is only in the town what is the effect here." Abhi said, "There may be an effect now or than today or tomorrow you or me or anyone can't say anything."Dev said, "Oak, Sir I will do what you say." Saying that he left the room

On Tuesday he went to his department, and his professor Rajesh called him in the office. Dev went to the room of Professor Rajesh. Dev said, "Sir, you called me." Professor Rajesh said, "Yes, Mr. Dev I was looking at your assignment your work quite improved." Dev said, "So sir, can I participate in the seminar." Professor Rajesh said, "No you cannot attain the seminar." Dev said, "Why sir, you can't do this to me."Professor Rajesh said, "Whatever it is, but I can give you a chance to prove yourself write a thesis about Romantic critics written by Professor Samal Bhattacharya of Oxford." Dev said, "If I write about that you will give me a chance to attend the Seminar." Professor Rajesh said, "off course I will do it."

Dev came out of his department and went to Sam's house. Sam said. "Hey,How was your day." Dev said, "Good enough." Sam said, "I am having a bit of rum and whiskey please do not mind." Dev said, "Go ahead what is there to mind." Sam said, "So what your Professor said you today." Dev said, "Nothing just poking me." Sam said, "For what?" Dev said, "he said if I write a thesis about romantic criticism then he will give me a chance to attend the seminar." Sam said, "Romantic critics arequite tuff." Dev said, "Let it be no problem for that." Sam said, "Whose Romantic critics." Dev said, "I will tell you after sometime, but first tell me your view about girls."

Sam said. "Girls what can I say." Dev said, "You wrote many books about romance you know that very well." Sam said. "I can say but an important thing you must remember." Dev said, "What." Sam said. "Entry towards a lady heart is an unexpected thing in an unexpected time."

Dev said, "Then it's great you can help me out with my assignment." Sam said. "But about what you didn't said the topic." Dev said, "Romantic critics." Sam said, "About whom." Dev said, "Romantic critics about Professor Samal Battacharjee." Sam said, "No I cannot help you in this matter."Dev said. "But why it's your work you can help me why are you doing it with me." Sam said. "I can't say you anything."

Dev said, "Fuck you, Sam! You want to know what the real bullshit is. How about you let me take it on this one because you're too damn scared to walk out that door and do something for somebody else. You're too damn scared! That's the only damn reason." Sam said," You don't know a goddamn thing about reasons, there are no reasons! Reasons why some of us live and why some of us don't! Well, fortunately for you have decades to figure that out." Dev said,"What is the use of writing so much, a cabinet full of books and the shut you locked it up" Sam said." There are questions which doesn't have any answer and that one of them." Dev said, "Alright you don't have any answer whatever I don't want any answer from you I know you have no answer". Sam was quietly sitting in his rocking chair and was speechless. Dev said, "Good bye."

Dev went to his hostel in a sad mood, he was sitting in his room and was looking outside the window to the Bhuban hills, and these hills have a mythological history of Mahabharata. It was a rainy evening, the month of June a rainy season in Assam as well as in the North East regions. He was looking in the mountains the trees and a small nearby village. The clouds were falling in the hill top as it want to grasp the mountains like a giant, and the drops of rain falling in the branch of trees of the forests, the dim of the street lights can be watched with the drops of rain in a dazzling way.

At that moment Panna knocked at his room, Dev opened the door and said, "Panna come inside, sit." Panna said, "Dev da you are bringing chicken tonight." Dev said, "yes, you come and join me five of us will have chicken together." Panna said, "I would like to have but my stomach is not so well today."

Dev said, "No problem you have 1 or 2 pieces oryou may have the leg piece" Panna said. "But they cut the leg piece because only for you." Dev said, "No problem I say Remash to cut two leg pieces for both of us". At night its 9pm five of them gathered in the dining hall. They started to eat their dinner with dal rice with some potato fry with chicken. Panna said, "Dev da do you visit to your teachers' house." Dev said, "Which teacher". Panna said. "That old man." Dev kept quiet for a moment and said. "Sometimes I do." Panna said, "Ok." Dinner was over and everyone was on the way to go to sleep. Dev said, "Ok good night." Panna said, "Good night Dev da it was a very delightful treat."

Dev went to sleep and was thinking about Sam why he did not gave his work to him what he was saying to him that many question does not have any answers. He felt that it was not right for him to talk in such a way what he spoke to him. Sam on the other side sitting in his rocking chair with a glass of rum and thinking that he should give his works to Dev whether he will go to him or Dev may come in his home again, but Sam was sure Dev will come to him and he will talk with him. It was 1 am, a call came to Dev's hostel, the night guard received the call, and the call was form the girl hostel of the University. At that moment Dev was coming to the dining hall to take some water from the filter, the night guard his name was Ramu a boy from Sikkim told him. "Dada, your name is Dev." Dev said, "Yes" Ramu said," Actually a girl from girl hostel was calling you." Dev said, "Why me?" Ramu said, "I cannot say one of your friends named Priya is very sick and there is no one present in the hostel their warden is also absent." Dev said. "You can't say it is not the time to leave the hostel our warden is also not present here." Ramu said, "I told them I can't understand what they are saying." Devi said, "Ok but it is very rainy tonight how can I leave without the permission to the girl's hostel." Ramu said, "what can I say Dada." Dev said," ok 1 will leave no problem you accompany me the warden is also not there so there will be no problem, come lets go do you have the torch with you." Ramu said. "Yes I have."

Dey went to the girl hostel, he saw his friend Priya was laying on the bed and some of the girls in the hostel were standing beside her. Dev came towards them and said,"What had happened to her?" Nazima said, "She was pregnant and gone through an abortion without the permission of the doctor and this led her to fall sick, she is in a serious condition right now." Dev said, "How it happened, who is the person behind it?" Nazima said, "A local boy who lives in that nearby village she was in a deep love with him and it caused her life." Dev said, "Deep love really, I think she proof her love in this act, Where is the boy right now." Nazima said, "Dev please do not joke, he ran away no body found him, we had reported an FIR against him the Dargakuna police station, they are doing their job let's see what happen." Dev said, "I am not joking, Priya made her life a real joke and how she gone through an abortion, did you call her parents." Nazima said, "Ok you do not be angry, she gone through this process of abortion by watching the website in the internet and this caused her to be in danger, yes we called them, they will come by tomorrow from Jorhat." Dev did not want to stay there for any moment, he wanted to leave that place as soon as possible, at that moment the warden came and Dev said, "Now I have to leave." Nazima said, "Why." Dev said, "If the warden saw me than I might be in problem, no you please take her to the hospital, I will talk to you later, good bye." Nazima said. "Ok, thank for coming, bye".

Ghostlike, wind was floating in the hilly place Dev was moving towards. his hostel. The wind was encircling the trees, of the hills, seeping languidly through the flowering shrubs. When he went to his hostel he was thinking why this person does such a big mistake in life which could affect their life, maybe it is their problem they should think what is right for them.

Next morning he went to Sam house, it was Sunday, he was knockingthe door of Sam's, and Sam opened the door. Sam said, "So you came I was waiting for you." Dev said, "I knew that you had been waiting for me." Sam said, "you were in need of my Romantic critics here it is takeit, hope your professor would like it." Dev said. "But why you did not gave me it before when I was in need for it". Sam said, "I can't say that but you listen I promised my wife not to give it to anybody but I cannot let it I can't see you feel sad about it, I gave you it forever." Dev was stunned; he cannot understand what to say. Sam said, "Dev sit with me lets discuss about the history of English literature, do you know anything about it."Dev said, "Something but nothing." Sam smiled and said, "Write few lines about two stages of English literature." Dev said, "What two stages."Sam said,

"Yes, write, Classicism and Romanticism." Dev said. "What is that please explain." Sam said, "Classicism-Criticism of life and humanism, and Romanticism-imaginative interpretation of life." Dev said, "I understood." Sam said, "What you understood." Dev said. "Tell me the next chapter." Sam said, "Study, go and study this in your hostel." Dev said, "Oak oak tell me the next one." Sam said, "Do one thing I am giving you this book write this sentence in this page." Dev said, "Where are you going?" Sam said, "Vodka time dear please do not mind." Dev said, "What." Sam said, "I am going to have a glass of vodka I think you may not like that, so I am going to my room to have it and come here soon." Dev said, "You have it in front of me I will not mind." Sam said, "It is not right you are a kid." Dev said," so what." Sam said, "Whatever I will not drink here, I will come after 5 to 10 minutes you keep on writing."

Dev opened the book and started writing the passage:

Emergence of English literature

6 century old English literature by Anglo section came from German 10664D Norman (French tribe invaded England), they used to speak in French and write in Latin this was the language of aristocrats Then came Chaucer father of modern English language. He borrowed French ideas of three types.

1. *Allegory*

2. *Romance*

3. *Vowel.*

He wrote the sentence and was waiting for Sam to come, after a few minutes Sam came and sat in his chair.

Sam said. "Here I come, your writing is over." Dev said, "Yes, I finished my writing." Sam said, "Let me have a look." Dev said, "Every thing is all right." Sam said, "Yes, good you are doing quite well." Dev said, "Sam can I ask you a question." Sam said, "Yes, why not please say." Dev said, "Do true love happens only one time." Sam said, "Ha ha ha, what happened why you are asking me so." Dev said, "nothing, but, there is something I did not said you, but you told me everything of yours." Sam said, "what was it about, does anything hurts you." Dev said, "Yes till now I cannot say but it does it hurts and I cannot say." Sam said, "what is that what happened to you, any problem." Dev said, "Yes something is wrong." Sam said, "Please share with me." Dev said, "2 years back when I first came to the university I was feeling very bore in my hostel as I do not want to talk with any one accept my two roommates, I was first of all given a room with Panna and Taiwan." Sam said, "I heard the name of Panna, you told me earlier but who is Taiwan." Dev said, "He was a boy from Manipur now he left the university." Sam said, "allright, than what happened." Dev said, "one day I went to Silchar town it was very late and it was 9 pm. I thought how can I reach my hostel that night I should stay in the town, but where could I stay. I was standing near in the bridge of river Barak, suddenly there was a heavy shower, I can't understand what I could do now. At that moment I saw a car coming towards me, the car stopped a girl between 25 years of age open the door of the car and told me to come and sit inside. I was stunned and got inside the car, she was so pretty I can't imagine, she took me in her house and told me to spend the night in her house. The next morning when I got up I was in the preparation to go to my hostel she offered me a cup of tea, and she startedasking about me, but I was quite I drank the cup of tea and came out of the house to my hostel, the night was a dream for me I cannot sleep because of the beauty that I saw in her, as if the rainbow in the rain, the moonlight covers the earth, without a drink a intoxication of her, her name was Mira, I always went to Silchar town to meet her in her house, She was a prostitute by profession. She said she lives alone in the house. When I heard that I did not wanted to stay in her house but leave soon as possible, but I can't do so is that for the respect of a women a very nice and a gentle young girl. I can't say that when she comes in front of me, I found a fresh fragrance of smell of soap in her dress; I do not know that compels me to take me in front of her. One day I said, that I love her, but she was silent and grasped in my shoulders and I lost the control of myselfthan I could not say what happen, she locked the door and took me to the room kissed me and we both were in the word of pleasure, her body was as beautiful as an adult movie actress, but, the next day when I came in her house she left a letter for me." Sam said, "Letter what kind of letter." Dev said, "Here is the letter Sam I always keeps it with me, thinking that she is with me." Dev took out the letter from his bag and gave to Sam. Sam opened the letter and started to read it,

Dear Dev,

I am leaving, I cried last night very much for you I did not wanted to leave you, but I did

not know why I did so. Whatever happened between us, I cannot explain, however someday I shall find some conclusion, which would be enough for both of us. In life we keep meeting new people and new stories are made and with each new experience, we understand things a little more a little better, love is like a vacation, it happens every year and it happens in all our life'sbut every vacation has its own charm, its own intoxication and we cherish them all as I cherish you, take care.

Yours
Mira

Sam read the letter, and was quite for a moment and said. "Think it was a temptation which came and went away." Dev said, "Ok Sam it's time to leave tomorrow is my seminar I have to prepare my paper that you gave me." Sam said, "So you are leaving." Dev said, "I will come tomorrow." Sam said, "If tomorrow you do not find me than." Dev said. "You started again, I am leaving good bye." Sam smiled and said, "Good bye Dev."

Dev went out of Sam's house, towards his hostel. Next morning he went to his University and presented his paper, everyone including the professors who were present there was so surprised to hear his presentation everyone stood up and clapped their hands.

After the presentation he went to Sam's house to say it was a lucky day for him it was only for Sam. He went and started knocking the door; Sam was not opening the door, after a second he saw that it was locked. He thought that he may have gone for a walk or to the nearby market, he waited for him but he did not return.

After 4 Months

It was the last day of Dev in the University and in the Hostel, because the next day he has to leave forever. He was in his room packing his bags to leave the next day. At that moment the cook called him. Dev, "are you there." Dev said, "Yes Kaku what happened." The cook name was Subash, after that another cook named Ramesh came everyone loved Dev very much. Subash said, "A man came in the ground floor asking about you." Dev said, "Who." Subash said, "I cannot say I saw him the first time." Dev thought may be Sam, he was so happy that he will see Sam after a long time. He ran to the down stairs, and saw a young man. Dev said, "Who are you?" The man said,

"I am Ravi are you Dev." Dev said, "Yes, you study in this University." Ravi said, "No I am a lawyer, I came for professor Samal Bhattacharjee." Dev said, "Where is he?" Ravi said, "He died 2 months ago in London, he was sufferingfrom a brain tumor quite a few months, he left the keys and a letter for you and a legal note that his house where he was staying belongs to you." Tears were falling from Dev eyes, he took the letter and went out of the hostel in the ground, where he and Sam used to sit in the branch and talk together.

Dev opened the envelop and started to read the letter.

Dear Dev,

It was a mistake to make this trip. I thought it would help me once again, that I saw the things Rita and I saw together. I miss you and I am sending you what I wrote last night before I left. In this way, I can come closer to you with my thoughts. Why the silence in the building does seems so life less to me, so queasy and desolate, so completely vivid without charm? I left that day without an explanation and did not come back, and you will also know that I have remained incommunicado. I am fine, nothing happened to me, but when the day's end I had an experience that has changed a great deal. I must simply ask you to accept my abrupt and unexpected act. You know me well enough and it happens for somewhat irresponsibility and in difference. Someone I once knew wrote that we walk away from our dreams afraid that we may fail or worse yet, afraid we may succeed. You need to know that while I knew so very early that you would realize your dreams; I never imagined 1 would once again realize my own. Seasons change young man, and while I may have waited until the winter of my life, to see the things I've seen this past year, there is no doubt I would have waited too long, had it not been for you. When we leave a place we leave behind the marks of us and that we can find it by going there, the marks of the girl Mira whom you meet 2 years back left the marks of love in you, and if it comes to me the marks of friendship, thank you for being a part of my life.

Yours Friend
Sam

Dev remained silent for a moment; Birancy came towards him and said, "What happened?" Dev said,

"Can't stop the tears." Birancy said, "nothing will happen smile I understand, come let's play cricket it's our last match." Dev said, "No I will not play." Birancy said, "If Sam was there he would not liked it." Dev said. "Let's go call all of them." Birancy said, "Great, come on man."

5

The Moment

It was the last week of May. The end of hostel days of Dev Sen Gupta. Dev was a student of Philosophy Department in Assam University, Silchar. The year was 2011, two of his friends after their dinner was sitting in the balcony of the hostel and were discussing among themselves, the time was 10 pm. Birancy said, "hey David tonight there will be totally dark I think the light will not come today." David said, "Dev did you call the electric office." Dev said, "Yes, I asked the warder he gave a call." David said. "Then what he said." Dev said, "He said that due to the storm occurred this morning there will be no electricity for the night, it will remain dark, and we may get electric facilities the next morning." David said, "Alright let sit and have a talk." Three of the friends were sitting and started their discussion."

David said, "Dev did you went to Silchar to meet your teacher Dr Maya Sen." Dev said, "Yes I meet her, the work is done for my project." David said.

"So you are leaving tomorrow." Dev said, "No, I am leaving day after tomorrow at 11 am." Birancy said, "I heard about your teacher Dr Maya I heard that she was suspended for a homosexual act from the University." Dev said, "Yes, but it was not right." David said, "Every one saying the same thing what has happened to her." Dev said, "I was in her house for 2 hours, it was not right what we say and think about other, stop it lets discuss about other things." Birancy said, "No Dev we want to know what has happened." Dev said, "than listen she said her husband used to beat her everything she was divorced, she stays all alone in her house one girl used to come in her house for work she used to send time with her and she fallen in love." David said, "Ha ha I think her husband knows, she was a lesbian for that she was divorced." Dev said, "Do not make fun of anybody like that David, you know damn about love." Birancy said, "David please stops." David said, "I am sorry I was wrong." Dev said, "I know even I was wrong too when Dr Maya told me love is a beautiful word but we people make it sounds very dirty why I do not know she said she will meet someone when after the world goes to sleep." David said, "Than." Dev said, "I asked her if she was not really happy with her husband is because he always used to beather." Birancy said, "Than what she said." Dev said, "No her husband used to love her very much but she always remains busy with her books and all and then she was a boring wife for him and then she got divorced." David said, "tragic, I thick her husband left her because she was a lesbian." Dev said, "David may be she was but it happens." Birancy said, "What happens?" Dev said, "Love happens we do not know howand when but with whom but it happens what Dr Maya told me."Birancysaid, "She is alright." Dev said, "I saw her she is well tomorrow I will goto Silchar to meet her again before I leave the University." David said,"Ok it's already too late let us go to sleep." Dev said, "Good night."

Three of the friends went to their room. Next morning Dev went to Silchar to meet his teacher Dr Maya. He knocked her door of her flat she opened the door. Dr Maya said, "Come Dev I was waiting for you." Dev came inside and sat in the furniture. Dr Maya said, "you came you please have lunch today with me." Dev said, "Madam I love to have lunch with you but I have to go to my University I am leaving tomorrow." Dr Maya said, "I know you are leaving for that I am saying you, who knows if I meet you in the future." Dev said, "I will have lunch with you madam."Dr Maya said, "Wonderful."

They both had lunch. Dr Maya said, "Sit for a while take some rest." Dev said, "No madam I think I should leave now or it will be late." Dr Maya said, "Ok I know you will leave but after sometimes it is raining now you just have taken lunch right now take some rest then when the rain stops you may go." Dev said, "Oak." Dr Maya said, "I am all alone in my house no body to share my thoughts and all." Dev said, "It was not right madam what the University did with you." Dr Maya said. " leave that topic I do not want to hear that I have something left for me after five months I am getting retired I am thinking after getting retire I will go to London people like us can live happily there." Dev said, "You loved that girl." Dr Maya said, "May be I said you one day you people do not know the meaning of love, love is a beautiful word but you all sounds like dirty I do not like that I think I will meet someone when one day when the world goes to sleep."

Dev said, "the rain has stopped I think I should leave now." Dr Maya said, "Oak you know my number if any problem you call me." Dev said, "Oak madam." Dr Maya said, "When you will fall in love you will understand." Dev smiled and said, "May be, bye Madam."Dr Maya said, "Bye Dev always is happy."

Dev came out of her house and on the way to his University. At that Moment it again begins to rain Dev had no choice but he entered into a hotel one girl came toward him and said. "Your name is Dev." Dev said "Yes do you know me?" The girl said "no actually I read one of your book my name is Priya" Dev said "Great it is nice meeting you Priya" Priya said, "I always wanted to meet you and today it is the time." Dev said, "I was going to my university and suddenly it started to rain." Priya said "You study in Assam University." Dev said, "Yes and what you do." Priya said, "I run this hotel." Dev said, "I am leaving tomorrow and it is raining so heavily I do not know what I should do." Priya said. "If you want you can take rest for some time. Dev said "No it will be not possible" Priya said. "I can do one thing I can drop you to your University by my car." Dev said, "Why you will take a lot of trouble for me." Priya said "No it's my pleasure I am a very big fan of yours." Dev smiled and Dev got into the car of Priya and they were all the way to the university it became really dark. The car got stuck in the road; Priya said to the driver what had happened the driver said it may take a little bit of time because the one of the tyres had been licked. Dev said. "I think it will not be possible for me to reach the University today Priya said, "do not worry I am there everything will be fine, it's raining heavily let me take a rest house for some time the driver will take a little bit of time to start the car." Both of them went to the rest house and entered a room Priya was completely wet due to the raindrops over her body the same situation was also for Dev. Dev said, "Priya you are completely wet you may fall sick." Priya said, "I know I think I should change and also youare also completely wet. Dev said. "I think you please go to that room and change your clothes I will change it here" Priya went to the next room to change her clothes and came out with wearing an erotic dress, Dev words got struck for a moment. Priya came in front of him and said, "Are you fine." Dev said, "May be I am but not so." Priya said, "Do you want to hear some music you will feel good, see there is a radio, now it is the time for good western music I always used to listen that when I am in my house." Dev said, "I love to listen."Priya switched on the radio and the music got started Dev heard this type of music of the first time. Dev said, "Priya can I dance with you." Priya said, "I love to dance with you."Dev said, "Not any romantic dance but something else Priya smiled and said, "What?" Dev said, "Lap dance." Priya smiled and said. "It would be my pleasure." Dev was sitting in a chair and she was giving him an erotic lap dance, the lap dance is such that a man sits or stands and the girls provide him with full sexual pleasure in the sexualparts. It was the first lap dance experience for Dev. Priya's ass was pressing the penis of Dev from the back. Dev pants budge up he touched the shoulders of Priya, he kissed on her shoulder and opened her dress, and he graved her back and pulled her toward him now he could feel her vagina through his penis. He kissed her on her lips. She was having very beautiful boobs like the porn stars which he used to see in the movies. He sucked her boobs but he was not satisfied by that he lay on the bed and told Priya to try the best porn moves she ever know. Priya was over him with full control in the Diamond in the buff position and fucked him hard from above. He was thinking to go for the missionary position but afterwards he thought no need of that, he told Priya to turn her back and he started fucking her from the back in the doggy position he fucked her as harder like a cheap dog, it brought the juice out of him and fallen over her. It was after 1 hour they came out of the room, got into the car and went to the University. It was about midnight. Dev said, "Priya I am leaving tomorrow." Priya said. "I know that Dev." Dev said, "I will come after 5 months to meet you and I will talk with you over phone." Priya said. "Take care Dev bye".

5 months later

Dev came to Silchar to meet Priya in her hotel. He did not found her there he asked a man staying there he said. "Where is the girl Priya? I have also gave her a lot of call but she did not received my call." The man said. "She is dead." Dev was shocked and said, "how when it happened." The man said, "She was pregnant and gone through an abortion and she did not wanted to trouble the boy by whom she got pregnant. She gone through an abortion and that caused her to dead." Dev was crying and went to Dr Maya's house, Dr Maya opened the door and was very happy to see Dev again. Dev told her what had happened, Dr Maya said, "forget that Dev it happens live in the present she was someone who taught you what love is it happens when and how no one knows but it happens, you remember the moments when you was with her, I am leaving tonight to London and I will miss you, you are one of my best student. I am leaving but when I will get time I will call you in your phone you also keep contact with me Dev." Dev said, "I should leave madam now, madam can I take a picture with you." Dr Maya said, "With me off course."They took the pictures. When he came out of the house it started to rain. Dr Maya said. "Bad luck and my good luck I will get some more time to gossip with you, sit and have a cup of coffee until the rain stops." Dev said, "Oak madam." Dev entered the house and it was raining outside.

6

The Autumn of Desire

June 2006

Assam University, Silchar,

Dev sen Gupta, research scholar from Assam University doing his research on Primitive Culture in the Department of Cultural Studies, is quite cold in Assam, due to the rain as winter is very near. Dev was lying in his bed and was thinking about a girl whom he liked most and talked with her online on face book, he thought a girl from his University doing her PhD in Economics loved him, but, when she blocked him from his face book account he then realize it was his illusion nothing is real in this world specially in his world. In his world nightmares comes true rather than dreams. A few moments later someone had knocked the door. Dev did not wanted to open the door as he was very much tired of his busy class schedule and want to take some rest, he thought no need to open the door let it be whoever is it will leave after wards. Again a few minutes later someone again started to knock the door, but it was not someone it was two persons. Dev has no choice but he opened the door and saw two of his friends were there, "what do you want." Dev asked. "We did not saw you whole day so came to know are you sick", Birancy said. Birancy was one of Devs friend in the hostel. "I was also thinking the same thing you know Deb, I was very much worried about you," David said. The other friend of Dev, both of them came to his room. "Let us go to the balcony and have a chat," Birancy said to Dev and David." "But now is 11 pm, you want to go now." Dev said. "Yes, let's go," David and Birancy replied together. After that three friends went to the balcony to have a discussion. "Hey Dev it is nice to be in the balcony," David said. "Why" Dev asked." "David is right Deb you can see tonight there is no electricity and I heard that tonight it will be dark and the light will not come, there have been a power cut in our University," Birancy said. "It is because of the storm this morning, there is flood in Silchar town." David said. "Yes I also knew that, I gave a phone call to the electric office just before 1 hour they also told me the same thing," Dev said. "Alright let's sit and have a talk," David said. Three of the friends were sitting and started their discussion.

"Dev did you went to Silchar to meet your teacher Dr Maya sen," David asked to Dev. "yes, I meet her, the work is done for my project," Dev said. "I heard that your teacher Dr Maya has been suspended from the University because of a homo sexual act in the University campus at night," Birancy said. "Yes but it is not right," Deb replied in an angry way. "Everyone saying the same thing but what had happened to her," David said."I was in her house for two hours, it was not right what we say and think about others, stop let discuss about other things," Dev said. "Dev tell me about the girl in Economics department with whom you used to talk on Face book", Birancy asked."Yes, I used to talk with her but she blocked me," Dev said. "Blocked you why, we thought she liked you so much and the article you wrote recently,I remember it was also been published in an edited book, from one University in Russia, your title was Harvard experiment in USA, she was very much impressed with your work," David said. "I know I wrote that it was a Harvard psychologists, on 1959–62, led by Henry A. Murray, conducted a disturbing and what would now be seen as ethically indefensible experiment on twenty-two undergraduates," Deb said."Why she did so", Birancy asked. "May be she had her own choice," Deb replied. "Did you go for tuition to teach a girl of 18 years you used to go there earlier," David said. "No," Deb said."But why," Birancy asked."I do not want to say", Deb said in a low voice. "Please say if there is any problem," David said."If any problem does not occur so I came from that place," Deb said. "What problem, tell us."David said. "One day when I was teaching the girl her name was Srija she told me that she had fallen in love with me," Dev said. "It's ok she is a kid, you make her understand that," Birancy said. "I told her but what happened I cannot explain you next," Dev said. "What happened?" David asked. "She told me that she love me, I told her to study, suddenly she kissed me on my lips," Deb said. "I cannot believe it, than what had happened," Birancy asked. "I was really confused I scolded her, told her I will leave and never come back but she cried and said sorry, I thought it was ok for her I did not understood I sat with her for her lesson after that she slowly touched my penis but I cannot control myself, she told me touch my breast for a moment I touched her breastand she became very much horny and pushed me, in the bed and gave me a blowjob, that was my first blowjob, I undressed her,she told me to finger her pussy and I did so and it took her breath away," Dev said. "Then what else happened?" David said."I told her it is enough I cannot do it, it's wrong," Dev said. "Then she stopped," Birancy said. "No, she did not stopped she told me she is virgin and she want to break her virginity by me, she got over me with full dominance and fucked me in the Diamond in the buff position as much as she can do it. Then I kissed her she kissed me I saw her body as beautiful as the porn star, I cannot say, I cannot control myself I cum over her," Deb said. "It's a very shame full incident," David said. "I know but I don't know one thing at that time I have fallen in love with her, when the girl from Economics blocked me I was upset I do not know whom to talk with, but Srija loved me from the day when I meet her near the lake, when I used to come in her house to teach her, but did not understood that," Deb said. "I can understand your feeling s but why did you left her tuition you can go there and teach her," Birancy said. "How we both can face each other I get a call from her parent's everyday to come and teach her but I cannot say anything not even her," Dev said. "One thing I want to say you that the girl from Economics whose name is Punam I saw her last week going to her Professor Rajesh house," David said. "She may go to her teacher house to understand something," Dev said. "No everyone says that she is engaged in a sexual relation with her teacher and spends night with him," David said. "It's her life, let her do whatever she wants," Dev said. "I think you should go and meet Srija tomorrow, because she was also asking me about you," Birancy said. Dev was surprised to hear that, "You did not tell me about that before," Dev said. "I forgot to tell you that, I also thought, just she was asking about you, but I did not know what had happened between you and she, so I did not told you earlier, I am sorry for that," Birancy said. "It's ok Birancy Dev go and meet her the next day," David said. "I am going the next day," Dev said. "Now let's go to sleep, I think the electric connection will not come today, hope we get enough water in the bathroom," Birancy said. "I think Birancy do much masturbation all the time so I think he needs to go and wash his dirty dick in the bathroom," David said making fun of Birancy. Everyone started to laugh. "Ok, good night everyone," Dev said. They all went to sleep.

Dev went to his bed and was thinking about Srija, how she came very close to him, she loved him so much, he then remember his school days when he was in the school he used to love a girl named Megha Dutta, she was reading in class 6 and he was in class 12, both of them used to go to school in the same bus, but she did not liked him so much, as he was not so good in studies.Next morning, Dev woke up early and went to meet Srija house, actually Srija lives in Silchar and the distance of Assam University from Silchar is 10 to 15 kilometers. Silchar is a town in Assam, a state in north east India. Srija full name was Srija mukherjee, she lives in Silchar, her father was a professor of Assam University in the Department of Chemistry and her mother is a teacher in a public school in Silchar. Srija do not get much attention from her parents much so she remain busy in her own life, with her school, friends and studies, she became very close with Dev when Dev used to come to her house totake her tuitions, she finds him really caring, and want to spend her rest of her life with him. She becomes horny when Dev is near to her, and for that she thinks about him and masturbate when she is alone, she also use vibrator for deep pleasure and also watch Pornography so that she can learn the moves and do the same what is used to me done in porn movies and one day she did it.

Dev went to Srija's home and knocked the door bell, Srija's mother Rekha opened the door and was surprised to see Dev after a long time and asked Dev, "How are you so many days I and Srija s father was very much worried about you, her father also told you to meet him in his department but you did not went to meet him what is the reason behind that." Dev was silent for a moment he did not know what he should say, "I was little bit busy with some personal work and was sick for few days mam, so it was not possible for me to come here," Dev replied. "But you could have told us earlier, no message no phone calls," Rekha said. "I am sorry mam about it," Dev said. "Go to Srija's room she is there, today is Sunday her school is also closed," Rekha said. Dev did not want to go in front of Srija how can he face Srija after what they did at the last meeting but he went to meet her in her room. Srija was sitting in her room, when he entered the room, she was very happy to see him and also was very angry, she came and slapped him, Dev was not surprised about it, and he knows that he deserves that but at that moment. Srija said, "why you left me, you did not picked up my phone I went to your hostel to meet you were not there, what you think about me what happened between us it was a fun for you, do you know how muchI love you.""I am sorry Srija it was my fault," Dev said.Srija came closer to Dev and hugged him tightly, "never leave me alone Dev I love you so much," Srija said. "I understand Srija, I will never leave you like this, ok let's get back to some studies I think we need to study," Dev said. "Ok, but one condition after studies we will visit at the nearby café, I want to have a cup of coffee with you," Srija said. "I do not drink coffee," Dev said. "Ok, we both will have tea," Srija said. "Ok as you wish, now let's study," Dev said.

After 2 hours both of them went to a café. The café was located near a lake, it was located before Assam University the place was not so much crowded with people, it was a very quite area with a beautiful landscape surrounded by pine trees with a big forest, and also it was surrounded by hills, some of the local say during the month of October they have seen tiger roaming around the forest. However, some people say this place is haunted and some supernatural events also took place here, the local hear cry or sound of a girl asking for help, it has been said that 20 years ago a girl was raped and murdered in this forest by 5 men, and this girl move around this place and attack young men who passes through this way and have sex with them, if he can't satisfy her, she cut their private part. So the spirit of that girl is also roaming in this place so no one is allowed to move around in this place after 9 pm, and also some folklore are connected with this place. Dev and Srija went to the café and both of them ordered tea and started their own discussion. This was the month of October as people say it's the time for the tiger to come here. "Dev did you feel scared when you came here" Srija said. "No why should I be scared", Dev said. "Actually it is a very lonely place and very few people visits here may be it is beautiful but it has many stories to tell," Srija said. "Whatever, but let's not discuss about it, I do not like it", Dev said."Ok, no problem, but I want to ask you something Dev," Srija asked. "Say what you want to say," Dev said. "Can you always be with me, marry me," Srija said. "How can I do it now you are just 18 and I am 31 it is not possible now, I want you to study and be a successful person in the future after that if I live my lifeI we will get married," Dev said. "What do you mean you will live?" Srija said. "I just said, nothing serious," Dev said. "Come Srija let me drop you to your house and I have to go to my University," Dev said. Dev and Srija went outside of the café to drop her home.

Dev dropped Srija in her home and was on his University. It was a rainy night, he entered the University campus and it was quite a far away from his hostel. After that he just went to a shop, which was in the University campus, the shop was very known to him and he always visits there to buy his daily things, he entered the shop and found the owner of the shop was sitting and smoking a cigarette, his name was Ramesh Chandra Das, he used to live there near the University and at that time no one was in the shop because it was at night and a rainy night. "Dev how are you come inside," Ramesh said." Hello Uncle I was just on my way to the hostel and the rain has started so I came here," Dev said." Very nice, I was also getting much boar so I got a chance to talk with you," Ramesh said. "No idea when the rain will stop I have to go to my hostel and have rest," Dev said. "Don't worry the rain will stop after a few minutes, is your project is over of Dr Maya, you went to her house," Ramesh said. "Yes I went to her it is over it is all done, "Dev said. "Did she tell you when she will join the department," Ramesh said. "No she did not tell me anything and also I did not asked her," Dev said. "How can she tell you she is upset," Ramesh said. "Is everything is true what others tells about her," Dev said. "Yes it is, but it's not her fault, she was in love," Ramesh said. "With whom," Dev asked. "With one of her students Punam from Economics department," Ramesh said. "What are you saying I heard that Punam was having a physical relation with her teacher Rajesh," Dev said. "No, I also got the same news, but it was not right, as I know, because one day I saw both of them in an intimate way," Ramesh said. "When did you saw?" Dev asked. "Last week I went to the University guest house to provide snacks and coffee, actually I got an order for the coming conference," Ramesh said. "I know about the conference after the conference she was suspended but it was last month," Dev said. "Yes you are right, I saw Dr Maya and Punam were together entering the guest house, I thought she was having any official work with her I thought they were planning for the conference but I followed them to their room, I saw they closed the door, so I thought why I should stay here because my work is over. So I was on my way to the gate of the guest house suddenly I saw from the window of their room they were kissing each other, I was down the building of the guest house, when I saw this I gone upstairs to their room, their door was little open I think in hurry they forgot to close the door," Ramesh said. "Then what you saw?" Dev said. "After that what I saw I cannot tell you, Dr Maya and Punam was kissing each other, hugs and kisses are falling like showers,both of them opened their dresses playing with their breastssucking each other breast giving pleasure by licking pussy, I came to know that they are lesbians,it was a feeling that theyboth love each other more than they love themselves, at that time I cannot stop mycum, even I masturbated watching this moment and I feel so sorry for it," Ramesh said. "Why are you feeling sorry it was not your fault, it's natural to all of us actually I even liked Punam I thought she is mature to understand my feelings but she blocked me on Face book, now I came to know that she is and always a Homo Lesbian," Dev said. "I think you know in this Assam University many teachers are having physical relations with their students, they have sex with them all night and give them what they needed, this University do not give good marks or grades to the students, it's a very sad thing," Ramesh said. "I remember one of my friend Debolina she was from Sociology department one teacher of us used to look at her in a very different way, Debolina used to tell me about him, but it was not the fault of the teacher but also her she was also very much interested in him, she always wanted he will have sex with her and she will enjoy that moment, now a days there is no taboo in this world", Dev said. "Yes it is true", Ramesh said. "I read a novel Jorashanko," Dev said. "Jorashanko is a place in Kolkata where Rabindranath Tagore lived," Ramesh said. "Yes, it was a very beautiful story, it was a love story of Rabindranath and Kadambari who was the sister in law of Rabindranath Tagore, it was said that Rabindranath was in love with his brother's wife, what is to be said in Bengali his *'Boudi'*, what is seen in the present Indian society love with elder brothers wife," Dev said. "I see, I have also read in North east Indian history Rabindranath Tagore that novel prize winner visited your state Tripura, seven times when Tripura was a princely state, "Ramesh said. "Yes you are right, the kings of Tripura love Bengali literature and culture so much and their official languages was Bengali at that time," Dev said. "What is this Kokbork languages from where it has came, I think it is a tribal language," Ramesh said. "Yes you are right it is the language of a tribal groupliving in Tripura, this language have a meaning, kok meaning verbal and borok meaning people or human, Kokborok is a Sino-Tibetan language of the Bodo–Garo branch. Kokborok was formerly known as Tripuri & Tipra kok, with its name being changed in the 20th century. The names also refer to the inhabitants of the former Twipra kingdom, as well as the ethnicity of its speakers. Kókborok has been attested since at least the 1st century AD, when the historical record of Tripuri kings began to be written down. The script of Kókborok was called "Koloma". The Chronicle of the Tripuri kings were written in a book called the *Rajratnakar*. This book was originally written down in Kókborok using the Koloma script by Durlobendra Chontai," Dev said. "Today I came to know many things from you and your state," Ramesh said. "Actually tribal and Bengali people live together but tribal think in many places of North eastIndia such as in Meghalaya, Assam etc, they consider the Bengalis as Bangladeshis because they migrated from East Pakistan that is now known as Bangladesh, at present, due to civil war, during 1970s." Dev said. "Ok, I see, now let's stop this chapter, lets discuss other things, tell me from where you came," Ramesh said. "I just came from my friend's house her father is a professor in this University, do you know him," Dev asked. "What is his name?" Ramesh said. "Her father name is Joy Mukherjee," Dev said. "Yes I know him well, he used to come in my shop, his daughter name is Srija," Ramesh said. "Yes you are right," Dev said. "Srija is a nice girl, I think you also go to her house for tuition," Ramesh said. "Yes I go, today I also came from her house, actually we went together in a café and had tea," Dev said. "Why you had tea in café, I know Srija likes coffee so much," Ramesh said. "Yes but I do not like coffee, so both of us had tea," Dev said. "That's nice, I think she likes you so much," Ramesh said. "May be, but I do not know this love have any destination, because she is very young than me," Dev said. "There is no age in love, she is younger to you not older to you, loves happens," Ramesh said. "Yes, it happen don't know if we will be together," Dev said. "Listen Dev, If love is written in ones fate, he will only find it, you will not find it, how many times you try, it is the game of fate and the journey of fate will come to an end when love is found. Like the rain are always accompanied by clouds, in the same way if she is yours, she will be yours forever, look the rain has stopped," Ramesh said. "Yes, I have to go to my hostel its late night now," Dev said. "Yes, good night," Ramesh said.

Deventered his hostel,and was lying in his bed and thinking the words from Ramesh, everything was true, this were the strong words that he ever heard from anyone, thinking this things the night passed.Next morning he woke up early, went to his department to meet his Professor for some research work, his Professor Silvia, was his PhD guide told him to go to a village outside Silchar town to collect some data, the town was located in a hill side know for Bhuban hills, this hills also has some historical story of Mahabharata anda temple of Lord Shiva is also located there, he was on his way to the hills so he thoughtto meet Srija and goto that place because it might take 2 or 3 days time to come from that place. So he went to meet Srija, everyone in their house was very happy to see Dev and Dev told them, that he is going to the Bhuban hills to collect data for his research purpose. "It's so nice I also want to go with you in the Bhuban hills," Srija said. "No it's not possible," Dev said. "No I want to go there please, I never saw that hills before," Srija said. "Ok, you can go after someday but not now," Dev said. "ok if you want to go than all will go," Joy said.Listening to her father Srija was very happy and also her mother said the same thing we all will go, so the same day they all went to the Bhuban hills and booked a guest house there, and started visiting many places.One day Dev and Srija went to the hillside to view the beautiful landscape, they were busy seeing the views of the mountains and plains andfeeling the beautiful air, at that moment there was a thunderstorm Sirja felt scared and came closer to Dev, "what happened to you Srija," Dev silently said. "No, just I thought rain is coming," Sirja said. "Rain is not coming it is raining, your mother told us not to come the weather is not good, now what to do, we may catch cold fewer," Dev said. "Do not worry so much see there is a small hut we can take some shelter," Srija said. Dev and Srija went to the hut for some shelter, the hut was empty as no one lived there for years, "Dev you did not think the hut is empty and beautiful," Srija said. "May be so what?" Dev said. "What so do you want to see my dance," Srija said. "No, I am not in the mood for dancing I am worried when the rain shall stop and we will leave," Dev said. "Just keep quiet, enjoy the moment donot worry sit," Srija said. Srija pushed Dev and he sat on the chair. "What are you doing Srija?" Dev said. "I am trying the lap dance for the first time," Srija said. Dev was speech less, Dev was having his first lap dance experience, and Srija was giving him the sexual pleasure. Srijas back was touching the penis of Dev, Dev pant budge up he touched the shoulders of Srija, he kissed on her shoulder and opened her dress, he graved her back and pulled her towards him, now he could really feel her from inside. He kissed on her lips, sucked her boobs.Dev was over her with full control and fucked her in the missionary position, it brought the juice out of him that fallen over her; both of them enjoyed the moment very much.After that both of them went to their guest house.Srija father and mother both came to know about Dev and Srija s relation that they are engaged in physical relations, they both were very angry on Dev and scolded him, threatened him to rusticate from this University, Dev was silent, "I love Dev so much and we both love each other, you cannot do any wrong with him, I beg you it was my fault," Srija said. "No, I will rusticate him from this University, and I have also talked with the Vice Chancellor of this University after we go to Silchar that is tomorrow, he will get his rustication letter," Joy said.Srija mother Rekha was quite, "Mom, you please say something, think about Dev," Srija said, crying and begging. "I cannot do anything," Rekha said. "Then I have no choice," Srija said. "What you want to do Srija?" Dev said. Srija said nothing and run away, went to the hills side and jumped from there, she committed suicide. Everyone came towards the hill side but no one can see her body was disappeared, in mist and in the bushes because no one can look down there it was completely dark.Dev was crying, cannot say anything.

15 years later

Dev completed his PhD from Assam University,and went to Massachusetts University, Amherst, USA,to complete his Post Doctoral degree, now he was working as a Professor inVisha Bharati University, Shantiniketan, Kolkata, West Bengal, India, a beautiful place build by Rabindranath Tagore,on 22nd December 1901, as he was not rusticated from Assam University becauseProfessor Joy and her wife didwhat theirdaughter told them, Srija loved him and they loved their daughter so they forgive him, but theyleft Assam University,they went to London after their daughterdied.Dev came to Assam Universityfor aconference andwas sitting alone near the lake it was an autumn where he and Srija first meet, and was thinking about her, actually Srija came into his life as a brand of dreams, but now only her memories remain, everything else that existed between them has vanished, he was wonderingwhy he stayed away from her, he never thought twice about calling her before, he couldn't break her heart even in a dream, he dedicated his life to her, but couldn't connect his fate, her memories remain in his heart eventhey both are not together.He was about to leave the place at that moment he meet a girl calling him from his back, "Hello Dev Hello hi how are you?" The girl said.Dev turned around, "Sorry do you know me," Dev said. "Yes I know you very well, I am Megha from your school do you remember me," Megha said. "Yes, Megha how are you I remember you I am a bit late I have to go to the airport after two hours I have a flight to Kolkata," Dev said. "Dev wait you are going to Kolkata I know I always read yours articles and always read news about you in newspapers I know you are working as a Professor in Vishwa Bharati University, Shantiniketan," Megha said. "Ok so what you want from me leave me alone," Dev said. "Why are you talking like this, I just came to meet you I saw you after so many years," Megha said. "In the school you did not liked me, you liked someone else," Dev said. "We were kids at that time you were my senior, how do I know what is love or likeness we were friends and I always respected you, ok I understandyou did not want to talk with me I am leaving," Megha said. "Wait Megha, I am sorry for being rude," Dev said. "It okay I understand, I know everything about you, you miss Srija," Megha said. "How do you know her?" Dev was surprised and said. Megha said, "Srija was my cousin sister, she used to tell me about you always actually she committed suicide but she knewthat she cannot live more than five years, but she did not wanted to die early," Megha said. "What do you mean me by that," Dev said. "I mean to say that she did not told you everything she loved you so much and she was sufferingfrom Bone cancer and did not wanted to tell you, she wanted to live each and every moment with you, but it was not possible," Megha said.Dev was crying listening to that, and fall down apart, Megha hugged him, when Megha hugged Dev, he could feel that fresh fragrance of smell coming from her body which he used to feel when he was in school, "it's ok do not worry she also told me that you worry so much please do not cry, Srija always wanted to see you happy," Megha said. "Ok, but what you are doing here," Dev asked Megha. "I just came to meet you, I knew you were coming here I saw it in the newspaper, you are an invite guest here and I also read your books and articles which are published worldwide," Megha said. "Ok, and what are you doing now a days," Dev said. "I am a Doctor, working in Calcutta medical college," Megha said. "That's nice, you became a Doctor, ok I am leaving I have to leave today," Dev said. "Wait even I also have to leave, we are on the same flight," Megha said. "Ok," Dev said. "Nothing is ok, see rain has started, there is a coffee shop and I know our flight is at night so we can have some coffee, sorry you do not like coffee you like tea," Megha said. "Srija said you that," Dev asked. Megha was silent, and said, "Yes, you said you have to go to the airport within 2 hours but I know your flight is at night and I am also in the same flight so I understand you wanted to run away from me." "No, it's not right what you are thinking," Dev said. "If it is, I want to have tea with you lets go," Megha said. "Ok, let's go for a tea," Dev said. They both went inside the café to have a cup of tea and it was raining outside.